CW00404561

Aurealis and Ditmar Awa
CHARLIE N

Charlie Nash was born in England and holds degrees in mechanical and space engineering, medicine, and writing. Her fiction has been shortlisted for the Aurealis and Ditmar awards. She lives on the eastern seaboard of Australia, and is working on two new novels, and a third Ship's Doctor installment.

   charlienash.net

f   authorcharlienash

Men and Machines I:
space operas and special ops

CHARLIE NASH

FLYING
— NUN —
PUBLICATIONS

FLYING
— NUN —
PUBLICATIONS

Published in 2019 by Flying Nun Publications, http://flyingnunpublications.com/

"The Ship's Doctor" first published 2010 in *Andromeda Spaceways Inflight Magazine* #47

"Dellinger" first published 2014 in *Use Only As Directed*, Peggy Bright Books

"Tartarus" first published 2013 in *Electric Spec*, Volume 8, Issue 2

"Deep Deck 9" first published 2012 in *Luna Station Quarterly* #10

In all the above first publications, stories originally credited to Charlotte Nash.

ISBN:
978-1-925775-09-9 (paperback)
978-1-925775-10-5 (eBook)

A catalogue record for this book is available from the National Library of Australia

Cover design by Richard Priestley

Contents

For all those who grew up watching Ellen Ripley and Sarah Connor and Dana Scully, and who played with Lego and rockets, and who never wanted to stop

THE SHIP'S DOCTOR

Adventures of Coryn Astridottir #1

This is the way it always ends.

My cheek burns from his stubble and blood rushes to my head. Got up too fast, but we're five minutes from port. I grope for my trousers under the covers. They're crunched down below the bed end, inside-out, cast off in a rush. I turn them by feel, then go after my shirt. *Be gone before he's back.*

I hear him cleaning up through the thin bathroom walls. He was good, this one, with his reactor-ore-etched nails and whip scars on his back. From the prisons or military chain-gangs maybe. I didn't ask his name. I never ask. Once my need is gone, it's gone. Then, I can let the other desire take over.

I can remember who I am.

I put a hand to the pod wall, cold from the space-soak. Two engines push us towards port: one a DM-starrunner, the other a MaximII. Their vibration thrills me, sending shivers dancing in my skin, a smile on my lips.

I interpret them while I pull on my trousers one-handed. The Maxim lags the DM, thrumming out of sync. Probably a coolant blockage. Nothing much fancy happens in the old gear. The pulse drive won't get much further than the return leg but it's not my concern. Some sap in the control room will see a red blinking light: this boat's only a red-class star freighter. A fast shuttle. I'll forget her before I've passed the airlock, just like the man in the bathroom. I never bothered to learn their names, because out there is the *Freya*. A blue-class mega station. Black shimmering crystal looming in the darkness.

After that, there's nothing else.

"Doctor."

A curt nod in khakis greets me at the entry dock. Stars on his shoulder say he's a second-captain, *Gibbon* stitched in white on his chest. Gibbon is a type of monkey, but I don't make the comment. It wouldn't help. Gibbon's a man whose humor evaporated into space years ago.

So I nod in return, take his hand firmly. "Captain."

He pauses just a bit too long. I know what he sees. Young woman. Too young. Too pink. Too pretty. But I forgive him that. He doesn't know. He licks sweat from his upper lip. The *Freya* is a big deal when you don't trust the physician. And he's old enough to think it's all bunk. Doctors for ships, new-verse crap.

No sense in jerking around.

"What is the nature of your problem, Captain?"

Gibbon's eyes flash left and right.

"Not here," he murmurs with a nervous glance to the crowds in the dock.

He turns on his heel and we're walking to *Freya*'s hub, waved through border control, on the long journey to the control deck. The *Freya* is the size of a planet-side city, like suburbs stacked one on another. She's a parasite station, hanging above Artemis, whose blue oceans are the only reminder of home. The Artemis system's the frontier of transformed worlds and *Freya* is the gateway. Space elevator. Captured asteroid miner. Terraformer. Bolt hole. My heels flash at the disgruntled crowds lining up with passports. I meld into the noise, following my monkey. They don't even scan my case.

The lift is a bullet in a tube, doors marked in red *Authorized Only*. Gibbon's fingertip glows with a red LED beneath his skin as his touch grants access. My desire stirs then; I want to touch it, feel the machine in the man, just as I itch to touch the walls and feel Freya's pulse. But Gibbon's a tense sort and there'll be time enough for astonishment. I am beginning to feel her anyway. Men like Gibbon barely appreciate what's in these walls. A new kind of thing entirely.

Two red bullets later, a blue-striped door declares *Operations*. Gibbon announces me, scuttles off. I've unsettled him and he doesn't know why, never will. Good for him.

The council of eight first-captains stands in a clutch. More khakis with loops of red at the shoulder. Ex-military men tending a sick giant. Giddy hens in a circle. The one with the extra gold bars steps forward.

"Doctor," he says with an inflection I don't like. His name is Murphy. I want to make a joke about the irony, but I don't. That part of my brain still works, but it's under control these days. Murphy introduces the others. I slide my eyes past their faces, not remembering names.

"What is the nature of your problem, Captains?" I press.

Murphy shifts in his shoes.

"First of all, I need to impress—"

I want to hiss. He thinks of legality and his ass before the station. I glance at his pants. No, not even an ass worth saving. But it's not him at stake. I give him a clinical smile, reassurance, no humor.

"Doctor-patient confidentiality was extended in the last verse approved regs, Captain. Don't worry, you're covered."

He breathes out.

"The core is fluctuating," he volunteers. *What the fuck do we know, you're the doc…*

I put down my case and turn to the wall screens.

"Bring me up the vitals, please."

A hovering tech engineer glides forward to man the controls. The old men don't get themselves dirty on the keys. Likely never learned to type. I'd do it myself, but I think faster this way. And I have to go through the motions, not to scare them first, and to let my connection find its frequency.

The tech's fingers dance. Data readouts fill the main screen, another scrolls graphs tagged in multicolored Helvetica. Colors grow and shift. No one in the room can read it; proprietary design. Nothing trips my pattern recognition, so I start on The List. I pine for direct connection, but I'm not there yet. My brain takes a while to scan the frequencies.

"Primary line pressure?" I begin.

I don't like this part; makes it seem like she's a machine, no respect for what she really is. I'm not a mechanic. But it does give the onlookers some comfort.

"Twenty bar median, ranging eighteen to twenty-point-five," answers the Tech.

His voice is calm, deep. Not bored. I like that. *Careful.* I keep my eyes on the screen.

"Normal then. Core field?" I continue.

"Half Tesla."

"Holding steady?"

"Blips two percent on a four-hour-cycle," he offers, matter-of-fact, professional.

I grunt. Unusual to get that sort of variation. I cast an eye at the techie's pocket. *Riley.* Strong hands. My brain drags my eyes upwards. Strong jawline too. *Please, not when I'm working.*

His eyes, an odd deep red, flicker to mine. He looks away quickly, with a small frown. Like he did something wrong. He avoids looking up again. His cheeks burn red like his eyes. He clears his throat.

"We changed out five filters in the last planet-cycle," he volunteers, staring at the wall.

"And?"

He licks his lips.

"And what, ma'am?"

"Why did you change them?"

He flushes. "The red light went on."

I nearly double take. No one goes by instrument panel anymore. But then I remember where I am. The furthest flung blue-class in the known verse.

"I need to see those filters," I say.

"Uh… they went to the recyclers."

I turn to stare at the first-captains.

"Gentlemen. You cannot destroy specimens. And you cannot put unchecked parts into the recyclers. This isn't a mechanical works, with parts that *break* and get *replaced*. She's a grafted organism."

"It's standard procedure—"

"I don't give a damn."

It snaps out of me, curt. Murphy shuts his jaw, squashing his cheeks.

"How long have these fluctuations been going on?"

"Forty planet cycles, give or take," says Riley.

"How long is that here?"

"About two Earth weeks."

"Two weeks?"

I glare at them. Dammit. They'd let her go for two weeks. The information brings a memory I don't want: of hot raw burn to my sinuses. I suck cooling air through my nose to forget.

"It took half that time getting you here," complains Murphy. "Anyway, I don't see the problem. There's a leak somewhere, a processor down, whatever. We haven't lost critical systems and—"

"*Time* is precisely the nature of your problem," I snap, mind doing the math. *Gods, two weeks*! "This isn't a leak, captain. A station this size can't maintain critical systems for two weeks on a leak."

I've folded my arms. My toe taps. I picked that up from my registrar at the docks and I've never shaken it. He even spoke to the ships that way. Time to take control.

"Riley, I'm going to need a sample."

"You going to explain what you're doing?" Murphy tries to re-establish authority. The other first-caps nudge each other, all that powder gray precision suddenly not delivering.

But I wasn't, not yet. They'd have their answers. But sharing information now will slow me down. I don't blame them; they're fearful. They remember the *Selenium*. She died spiraling into a sun, when the DNA microsplice tech was new. We all remembered her, because her doc went down with her. There were rumors about why. But this wasn't about that, not exactly. Riley and I have a date with *Freya*.

Riley keeps quiet at first. He walks beside me, along cleated maintenance deck grateways, a system the passengers never see. His manners change. Back straighter. Jaw set. He's not as green as I thought, just a show for the ops room. If someone had asked, he'd have said he was leading me to the core system hatches, but no one leads me anywhere on a ship. I could have followed her heart with my hand on the walls.

"So, what do you need a sample of?"

We stop at a bullet call point. Riley's thigh is long and muscled under the blue fatigues, which run a smooth line from belt to knee. *Not now.* I look at his face instead. Unlined, earnest. Interested. *Damn.*

"What do you know about the core?"

"Blue-class StarLiner Evo model," he says, like the fine print from the catalogue. His red eyes shine.

I pause.

"Not many people know that."

"Know what?" he asks. I wait as the bullet slides open and we step inside. The doors close.

"That the station's core defines its class, not its size," I say.

"Oh. My dad—"

He catches himself as the bullet whizzes away. My stomach drops before the magnos kick against the acceleration. My grandmother knew the man who developed the magnos. That still gives me a rush.

"What else do you know?" My eyes wander to his buttocks. They curve under the blue drill, muscled and hard as a synthetic melon. He catches me looking.

"Its proprietary… some of the guys in tech wanted to take one apart, see what was in there, but it's not supposed to be a good idea."

"That's right. Know why?" The bullet accelerates again.

"Because it's a living machine," he says softly.

"That's right." I close my eyes, put a hand on the wall. *A living machine.*

The exact details are secret, of course, but that doesn't mean I don't know. The Company spliced DNA programs with the micromachines in the core, programs that could copy themselves, evolve, be selected, multiply. Superior to anything they'd ever programmed in software. That made it possible to make a system for a blue-class that wouldn't be obsolete as soon as it left the dock. The hitches were years in development, but they were mostly about getting the signal out. No one had built ports for something that was living matter on a scaffold.

In the end, it didn't matter. In a few generations, the DNA machines built their own scaffolding onto microwires, massive bandwidth, parallel processing. But then the techs couldn't understand what went on inside. It didn't look like what they'd programmed anymore. They couldn't diagnose the problems.

Then they found out they didn't have to, not exactly. All they needed were us.

The ships' doctors.

We leave the bullet at the core deck. Riley swipes a glowing LED finger over the reader. I'm having a hard time keeping my attention off him. The strength in his hands, the stamina of a youthful body. Only the core room lets me forget for a while.

I put my case on the floor and pull it open. An old-style doctor's case with pouches, slots and hidden places. It smells of leather and Listerine. I get my tools. Fifty mil syringe and sixteen gauge needle in plastic packets. Swab and graft plaster. Gloves, goggles. Mask. I hold one out to Riley, which he takes with a confused expression.

"What do I need that for?"

"Because you wouldn't want to be sorry."

He shrugs and pulls it on. Obedient too. *Probably looks good in leather.* The urge is getting a long-nailed hold. I shake my head, trying to dislodge it.

I go to the walls then: thousands of four-inch square panels with quarter-turn fasteners holding them over the central exchange. From here, *Freya* sends her nervous system all over the station, even grows satellite control centers where they're needed. But this, right here, is the master.

I listen through my fingertips and finally I feel her frequencies resolve under my touch. My heart skips to beat in time with her, and the connection rush squashes my other urge. Our minds, such as hers is, speak. Our direct connection is nearly complete. And I feel her system choking. I follow the stress to a high point, then point to the panel.

"Here."

Riley gets his quarter-turn tool. I unwrap the syringe, tip it with the needle. He turns the four points with a practiced hand and the small window to *Freya*'s core stands open.

At first, it looks like a jumble. A gelatinous web, like jellyfish running with pale blue streams piled one on another: oxygen dissolved in inorganic medium. The look of it isn't right, but it wasn't what I was hoping for. On *Selenium* the microwires got an impurity and corroded. The sloughing debris poisoned the DNA and the whole system went down. Making calculations while sick and a-kilter, she ran into a sun, my colleague still trying to stabilize the poison. But if the wires were corroding, there should be rivers of red or black shot through the mix.

This is something else. Distributed, cloudy. I tell myself it's no big deal, but I still bite my lip, remembering. Because there was another station before the *Selenium*. One that never made it out of port.

One that got infected.

My breath steams my goggles as I plunge the needle tip into the cloudy goo. It's only ten mil under the thin membrane. My thumb moves the plunger by muscle memory, and a thick spurt of pale blue sits in the barrel. I withdraw, swab the spot and stick on the graft plaster. Riley has the panel on before I've capped the needle.

"Now what?" he asks.

"Analysis."

"And you're expecting what?"

He leans over me as I pull the mobile micro-bio unit from my bag. I try to ignore him, running a loving finger along the keypad. It's crude, limited range of species, but accurate. I load the sample cassette, click it home. The red light blinks, working.

I look up at Riley then. His hair – the color of burnt umber –

touches his skin like fronds of a willow hiding one strange eye. My hand moves to his leg.

The unit's light blinks green before I get there, and I turn the move into asking for a hand up. Riley obliges, grip firm and sure. My urge flutters uncomfortably, and I do what I never do. I hold his eye with mine.

"What does it say?" he whispers, breath hot and close.

"You have an infection."

The first-captains stare at me. One moves his mouth like a fish.

"I'm sorry, what?"

"You have an infection. *Pseudomonas astrolix* and *Radiosolis* virus."

Bugs born in the gamma radiation-soaked cold space, so far departed from Earth species it's like they never saw planet-side at all.

Murphy scratches at his armpit, beetroot fingers deep within starched khakis. Looks like he gets along with Gibbon.

Someone at the back pipes up.

"Is that a software virus?"

"Can they even get infected?" Their voices flutter into a rabble.

And Murphy comes to where I want him: impatience.

"Alright, ok. Infection. What do we do? Is it serious?"

I breathe out. Once they start asking for advice, usually things go smoothly. I melt a little.

"Can be, but you're fortunate. These cores have an immune system, too. She actually fights pathogens all the time. This infection's a bit more serious, but I'll find a suitable course of anti-viral and anti-microbe. Order it on the next fast shuttle. We'll shut down to critical systems. You don't want to maneuver. She'll recover."

I look around their faces. Relief, boredom, acceptance. House of monkeys.

I press forward.

"You know, this is pretty straightforward stuff. If you had a resident doc, you'd have had it sorted out a week ago."

At this, Murphy's face squashes into a disgruntled humph.

"We did," he grunts. "He died, that's why you're here."

Something wicked claws my innards. It feels like freefalling to planet-side, turning inside-out, drifting in space without a suit.

"When?" My voice is a knife, sharp, fearful. *Please no …*

Murphy shrugs.

"Just on an earth week ago. Space fever. Died in his bunk."

I hiss involuntarily. My teeth chill from the air rush. "*In his bunk?*"

"What?"

I force myself to be calm, pleasant. Make him forget the hiss. As pleasant as I can get. Space fever. Code for infection.

"Captain, order the station to quarantine."

"What? Why?" demands Murphy.

"Do it! I'll be back in an hour."

I grab Riley by the collar. "Take me to the doctor's bunk," I hiss.

The doctor's bunk is cramped and cluttered with journal papers and yellowing texts in piles and spilling from suitcases. I run my fingers across the crumbling sheets; not many use paper anymore. Dirty cups and a crumb-speckled plate sit atop the stacks on the tiny desk. Twisted-nail and holographic puzzles cluster in rows on a high shelf. Regs say the crew must wait a fortnight before they can dispose of his gear. That might save the station yet. The bed is still rumpled. A touch screen blinks idle over the bed.

"I need his notes. He would have recorded all he did."

I touch the screen but it asks for a print-scan and password. I swear at my lack of implants.

Riley moves close, his fingers replacing mine.

He glances sidelong as the system screen glows in our faces.

"We could have done this from operations," says Riley. The screen reflects in his eyes.

"No, not this. Records are confidential. Can't be stored on the central system. Has to be here."

Riley's hands move deftly, opening the personal folders, bringing up screen after black screen. From the side, those strange red eyes brim like red caramel. I wonder if he has grafts. But just the thought brings excitement and I look away.

"Nothing. It's empty."

"It has to be there. He would have recorded something like this."

He checks again. I feel the block between me and the system, an agonizing distance. I long to jack in but I've never allowed myself the hardware. I don't think I could stop.

Then I look around me.

"Riley. Stop."

"What?"

"It's not in there."

I begin on the stacks of papers. *Of course.* All the ship's docs have a problem with machine fascination. Some think it's because we want to get inside our patients. But it's more than that. It's addiction. The way your heart skips when you control something this big. The way the universe expands in hard-wire connection. And more, we all knew how much it could bring us unstuck. Unable to do our jobs. Useless. We took measures. This doc kept his hands off the machines even for records. My problem, my insistent urge, is a little shade different, but not much.

Riley thumbs through piles alongside me, the cabin keeping us close. I hold my breath because he smells of spice and machine oil and the round muscle of his shoulder shows through his shirt as he reaches under my arm. He comes up with a fat leather-bound notebook, pages edged in grime.

I take the book, breathing in grease and sterilizer, anchoring myself back in the realm of doctoring. I flip to the last entry logs, half-way through the pages. I read it under my breath.

Drive continues in flux. Edema in capillary supply lines. Suspect pathogen. Sample analyzer requiring part. Aspirate sent fast pulse to Poseidon.

"So?" asks Riley.

"He did the same thing. But the on-station analyzer's broken. He sent the sample on a fast shuttle to Poseidon. He wouldn't have dared start a treatment without the sensitivity analysis. This could be good news; we'll have that earlier than I thought..."

But he'd died. And there's something not right about that. My eyes scan higher. I flip back a page, past the station's early clinical signs. Then, I find another entry. I feel cold writhe in my skin.

I point to the date.

"When was this?"

Riley tilts the book, eyes narrowed.

"Um, two weeks ago. Just after the last supply boat."

"When was the next one?"

"It was today – your boat."

I hiss, the sound rising from beneath my soul.

I drop the log, and it falls open at the entry: *Last order not sent. Reordered masks.*

Riley meets my eyes. His pupils contract, understanding.

"He took a sample," he says slowly. "But he was out of masks."

"First rule: no mask, no sample. Not when you might aerosolize an infection, breathe it right into your lungs…" I speak right from the handbook, that first week in the docks.

Then the comms buzz Riley's tracer; it comes through on the overhead speaker.

"Doctor. We have an issue in med dock. I'd like you back in operations… please."

It's Murphy. About to learn his law.

With the station in lock-down, all door readers are set to red, but Riley's micromesh fingertip is customized to *allow*. We glide seamlessly through empty corridors, feet falling in step. There's urgency, doubled by my compulsion, which is starting to assert itself again. I curse it, but it's there. And I feel the pressure of company as soon as we're inside operations. Then I know I'm not going to be able to put it aside. It will grow until *Freya* is only at the edge of my mind, unable to perform my function, victim to my failing. And that's the only thing that's worse than the urge itself.

Murphy quilts his jaw while the other captains sit around the low table, crumpled gray faces above crumpled shirts. Riley is bright and fresh in the corner of my eye. I clench my teeth, holding onto focus.

"How many cases do you have, Captain?"

Murphy shifts in his seat.

"Four."

"Who are they?"

"Two émigrés serving waiting tables, staying the doc's room. And a cook, and a cleaner."

"Shit." I say it out loud. I never got the pre-processor implant, the one that lets you review messages sent to the speech center before they go out. I suspect Murphy has one. Right now, he probably wishes I did too. But a cook and a cleaner see dozens of people every day. If the station had infected the doc, the doc had infected the station.

To his credit, Murphy only raises a caterpillar eyebrow.

"How long till it spreads? What do we do?"

I sigh, allowing him to feel a little weight of the issue. But I try not to think of *spreads*.

"Seems a week for incubation. There's nothing to do. Stay in lock-down. The sample was sent, we have to wait for the sensitivity. You have a doc in the med lab?"

A *real* doc, that is. Murphy nods.

"Let him handle it. Alone. Minimize contacts. I'll handle the station. Go back to your quarters. The fast shuttle will have the answer here as soon as they can. I will monitor *Freya* with Officer Riley."

The captains are caught uncomfortable needing to take direction from another and there's a lull. But I've seen this before. It's quick, and then comes relief: doing *something* that feels so easy, much like doing *nothing*. They leave, a flotilla of military walks, stodged with age, emptying the halls and into the bullets. Riley turns his back to follow them.

I wait.

He glances back as he walks, a smile on his lips, red blush creeping down his cheekbones. I take just the moment to watch the hall, feeling *Freya* turn around us, her sickened soul filling the walls. The sensation blooms to full perception just then: I've made full connection. Blood rushes to my head and my lips tingle, like a moment in freefall, pure thrill.

And at least she's stable. Because now, the need is upon me, strong and unyielding. So, when Riley turns unhurried at the end of the hall, I follow.

This is the way it goes.

Riley's room is a standard issue gray-walled serviced cabin. The air is dry, with a faint musk that disguises the usual bouquet of cleaning chemicals from the bathroom.

He holds open the door. On the low shelves, a squat glass bottle is the origin of his smell; it's on his clothes, even on the rough blankets made to military precision on the bed. The small table holds a pile of yellowing paperbacks next to a wireless tablet, like a Zen garden. Uniforms, pressed and crisp, fill the slim tall cupboard, jeans and shirts stuffed on the shelves below. A digital frame on the wall scrolls photos; heavy military freighters in dock, Riley in civvies with a tall man, a bikini model I recognize from Poseidon. Two lives in the same cabin.

Riley presses the door closed and locks it with his fingertip. My pulse quickens at the glow under his skin, and the flash of his eyes as the light catches the edge of the grafts. He leans against the door.

"Nice place." I speak only to cut the air. Too much tension, it will be over too fast. He looks at me steadily.

"I've never met a woman like you before," he says, the blush creeping a little lower. He can't quite meet my eyes.

I tilt my head very slightly. "No, you haven't."

The cabin is small, we are very close. The scent of him grows stronger. I step forward. The low light glints off his red-blond stubble. We stand an inch apart. The air heats between us. His eyelashes dip as he glances down. His pupils expand so they become red rims, then contract to pinpricks as I cast a shadow on his face. *Nice.*

"Who did your eyes?"

"I don't remember."

"Fed forces?"

He doesn't answer but taps finger to thumb; the lights fade. I sense myself in green afterglow on his retinas. Those aren't passive grafts. They're clever parts with an AI that demands a link-up. My brain doesn't have a gate in that circuit and I can't turn off. Built to bond to hybrid systems. Men and their machines.

Our left fingers brush together and his right hand cups my head, tilting. I feel the connecting electro-nerve pulse sparkle. But I'm in long before he is. I brace, my fingers hook his back and I jack his mind through those eyes.

It is over, but he doesn't leave.

I lie in the crook of his arm, all heated skin. His fingers play idly on my shoulder.

"How old are you?" he asks.

I smile in the dark. *Freya* beats in the wall behind me, tiny pulses in her supply capillaries matching Riley's heartbeat.

"Old enough," I say.

He strokes my neck. He takes a breath to say something. Stops, and doesn't. Raises the lights just a fraction.

"Star Ops," he says finally. "My eyes."

I nod in the dim, looking up. His irises give a slight rainbow shimmer as he shifts from infrared back to light spectrum. It's a good job; the early grafts had no control, infrared all the time. I tell him so. He knows. Says his dad knew people.

"You don't have any machine splices. No implants, hybrids?" he asks softly.

"No. It's best I don't. I couldn't stop."

I sense him frown.

"Odd for a ship's doc. But you're not a clean slate, are you? What do you have?"

Perceptive. Have to be for Star Ops.

"Not implants," I say quickly. "Transplant. Autologous."

"What is that?"

I stifle a sigh. I am released now, and *Freya*'s presence sits heavy in my mind. Her cells vibrate with mine, like strings of one instrument. She is sluggish, but though nothing has changed with her, I don't like to linger. It is not for me.

I go to get up, but his hand closes on my arm. My hair tumbles around my face; its touch is odd, something I almost never feel.

"I want to understand," he says.

I try to shake him off, but he is persistent. Lapse of my judgment, I can usually avoid the inquisitive ones.

"Please," he presses. Asking, not begging.

I look him right in the eye. And my transplant finishes its connection to his graft. *Dammit.*

"A long time ago, when the techs were new—" I begin.

"In a galaxy far, far away?" he asks with a grin.

I stop, unsmiling. To his credit, he lets the grin fall. I'm not a roll to joke with.

We stare at each other, his grafted eyes glimmering. From our wireless connection, I see the image of me in his mind: pearly skin, with dark eyes he thinks are sucking at his soul. Genuine regret, genuine interest. I stop pulling against his arm.

"If I wanted to be a ship's doc like you, what would I need to do?" he asks softly.

I remember steel and a clean smell. Long ago. No time for the details.

"Have your neurons harvested. Then, have a bright tech sequence a DNA facilitation program"—I mesh my fingers together—"software for your hardware."

"Then what?"

"They go into the machine scaffold. Live with the grafted machine neurons. Learn their frequencies. Then, they go back in your head. You hear the machine."

"That simple, huh?"

"Of course not."

Spend a decade going crazy, before you get that first twitch. Watch the others around you dying five to one.

His eyes run over me meditatively.

"That what you're doing with me now? Listening to my machines?" he says finally, softly.

I find myself hostile. So I lie.

"No."

But there's a tenderness in his face. No. Some memory maybe. A look like something admired.

Then *Freya* sounds a warning. The vibration has changed. There is no siren, no voice on the speakers, but there's been a violation. At the docks. I put my hand to the wall.

"You know—"

"Shhhh! An alarm's been tripped."

Riley frowns.

"I don't hear—"

"The alert systems are disabled. Someone's in the system at the docks."

Riley's on his feet in an instant, naked before the console, his fingers flying over the keys.

"They've locked it out," he says. "Ops will be sealed. No, wait—" His eyes rake back and forth between shifting screens. "They're already in Ops… running a routine to override the quarantine."

I swear. "Why would Murphy—"

"It's not him."

Riley stands back from the terminal, turns his red eyes on my face.

"You familiar with military protocol, Doctor?"

I stare back at him. The station pulses messages in my brain; she already knows what Riley suspects.

"It's a coup," I say.

He nods. "And they've shut the port."

I slam my fist into the wall, letting her feel my frustration. That I'm still on her side. However much I neglect in my distraction. Because they'll be no analysis while there's no port, and no treatment either.

And she tells me more.

That they're trying to access the pulse drive.

"What the f——" Riley's seen it too.

But I am already out the door, clothes in my hands.

Riley stops me before I knock down the ops doors.

"There's ten guys on the other side that won't stop to ask who you are before they kill you."

I growl, throwing him off. *Protect the station.*

"I know ten ways to put you on the floor right now," he hisses.

I grab him back, snake my hand around his neck, thumb on his soft throat. I'm quick; he doesn't know enough about me. His red eyes shift spectrum in surprise.

"And *I* know three ways to make your eyes bleed without touching you." My own breath is hot on my lips. I wouldn't do it intentionally, but worse has happened to a system linked with me when I'm angry.

He backs off, but the doors are already open.

And a familiar voice reaches me from the depths of ops.

"Doctor, if you would, please."

There's a group of them, in space fatigues, camouflage in grays and shadows. I block the door, taking them in. The first and second captains are bound on the floor, diminished, under guard. And there at the front is the voice's owner: radiation etched hands, short blond military cut. I hold my face expressionless while underneath I swear a savage curse. Under that shirt are whip scars, and everything else I touched in his serviced shuttle cabin.

He grins at me, power and precision. No wonder he was good. Gun-runner. Do-no-gooder. I give him a cold eye. Then as I move inside, I see his shirt: pips on the shoulder announce him a commander. *Riley* stitched in red against the blue.

Riley starts in my shadow.

"Dad?"

What the f—-

"Good timing, Officer Riley," says the commander. *Ah, irony.* I feel Riley through his eye hardware in my senses. His signal is cold and confused; he has no part in it. The Commander nods and two heavies take Riley to the flight panel. "Now, if you please, we need a small orbit adjustment."

I move before I've thought, and the heavies block my path.

"You can't move the station," I say.

Riley's worked up too, kicking against the heavies trying to put him in a chair. "What the fuck did you do? Put a damn chip in my head? What? How'd you get in here?—"

They've soon got a gag on him. They tape his shoulders and ankles to the chair, leaving his hands on the keys. It looks like a spaghetti western, just without the train. My brain sees it comical, but there's no smile computed to follow.

I tilt up my chin.

"You can't move the station. The core's infected."

Freya fills half my mind. I notice the stains on the room panels, dirty marks on the floor beneath console chairs. I tap the feed from *Freya*'s video lenses, fuzzy and confusing in their overlay. I can't do multiple channels at once. Still, there are people moving about in the hallways, spooning food in the mess.

The images come into the display feed, and Riley gives me a despairing look, lips pushed into the gag.

No quarantine. We both know it.

"Commander," I stumble over my words, trying to be slow and clear. "Order the station back to lock-down. Do it now."

The Commander gives me a meditative look. Taps a finger along that perfect jaw, the same one he gave his son.

"You know, Doctor, that was a pretty clever move. Quarantine. Nearly gave us a right problem. Station gave you a heads-up, I imagine? Much harder to get out of the docks when there's a lock-down. But I need everyone in the Great Hall for the pictures when we send the demand. And I'd think twice about being so clever again."

He lounges in the first-captain's chair. The bound first-captains, miserably prone, stare from their eye corners.

"It's not about you," I snap. "The last doc passed the infection to the crew. Now you've got them milling about like pigs in a feed barn, happily infecting each other. The core's compromised. You can't adjust orbit under infected conditions. She could miscalculate and send you spinning into planet-side, get it?"

The heavies move in. One is bald, tattoo running over his ear. The other has acne scars on his cheeks. Like an old B-grade movie.

"You touch me and I'll run your brain out your ear holes."

Pity I need them a bit closer. I would have done it without thinking. Just having mindless twitchy thugs inside her ops, fingering their weapons, running grubby fingers over her keys while they lick their lips makes me wild and dangerous. At least Gibbon and Murphy have righteous intent.

"Enough, Doctor."

The Commander looms just out of reach. He's seen my wild eye. *Hasn't he just.* He dares to come close.

"My, wasn't our encounter fortunate?" he whispers. "Otherwise, I mightn't have known who I was looking for."

He is trying to shame me. He should know better. You don't learn about a person from half an hour in their bunk. I pointedly look at his crotch, and eventually he coughs, draws his weapon. He presses the muzzle under my chin.

"Now, you and my son are going to do a little orbit correction.

You better hope that you're as good as your reputation —- keep us from falling out of the sky. Because, when those feds come looking for us, like you know they will soon, they're going to have to look over half the damn sky."

He emphasizes the point with an arched eyebrow. I meet his gaze. His eyes are grubby brown, the kind that looked better in the low light. This is why I leave them behind. But his skin looks well in the dusky light. And my urge curls itself, remembering his touch. *Shut it, traitor.*

"The infection will spread to everyone," I grind my teeth, knowing it will do no good. "You won't have anything to bargain if they all die."

Pressure on the gun increases. He leans in, his breath hot peppermint. A bedroom voice. *Just a little closer.*

"I don't need them alive for long," he says and winks. Pushes me down beside his son.

I close my eyes, not in fear but because otherwise I might lash out and kill Riley with him: flick off that tiny switch they put between my amygdala and motor cortex and unleash the damage. But now they'll send guards to the hall to be infected, too. Some of them will live, pass it to the feds, who'll get on another shuttle… I squeeze my eyelids hard, pressing on the part of me in step with *Freya. Can you hear me?*

Riley's already got the screens moving, parsing through the pre-pulse checks. But he's going about it the slow way, burning time. We can't keep it up for long. The old man's not that stupid.

There's a hatch under my feet, Riley says.

His lips don't move. It comes to me from his hardware, like Freya's voice, all in my head. There's more behind those eyes, I knew it. Standard grafts do not transmit.

He counts to three and we duck. Don't know how he shifted the tape. Riley has the clips out before the heavies have reached for their weapons. I drop in a slither, synthetic pants on smooth vent chute. Riley loads seal charges as he falls, and the cover hits home with a zing of hot plasma. Commotion is suddenly far behind. I collapse legs as we hit the end and roll, but Riley lands like a sprung cat, with unnatural grace. He looks at me with those red moon eyes and I feel the pull of interest in another person beyond wanting to use their body for relief. First time in a hundred years. I look quickly away.

We're in the massive duct exchange, continuous dull gray panels. Tubes enter and leave made in foil lighter than air. A hard space. Our voices echo.

"We have to leave," he says, not breathless.

I recoil.

"I can't leave," I say, but my mind keeps going. You can't understand. What it's like to be jacked in, a servant to a being greater than yourself. Serve, befriend, command. Medicine between beings dissimilar, but similar enough.

"*You* don't understand," urges Riley. "He'll take down the whole thing. It's happened before. And if they find you, he'll torture you to get the station."

Freya vibrates within me.

"The escape pods are disabled anyway," I say.

He makes a face.

"There's still the shuttle in the dock," he tries.

I have to smile. "It has a coolant blockage in the MaximII, won't make return without parts."

And there's more. *Freya* shows me the pictures: the military shuttles jumping from Far Space, puffs of violet plasma marking the void. They're fast-pulse craft, they'll dock in less than fifteen minutes.

I turn to Riley, but he's already seen; our link is open broadcast already. *Dammit all. Not what I wanted.*

"We have to stop them. Infection will spread." I say it quickly, to cover *we*, it's foreign, unfamiliar, feels wrong on my tongue. Instead, I go to the air-light foil and tear it with a nail. Out on the maintenance deck, air rises in a choking furnace, heading for reconditioners. *Freya*'s skin feels wafer-thin beside me, her blue-medium pulsing oxygen to the core. I run for the core room, to pass the line I promised not to cross, to override the DNA programs. To take her over, a child's mind corrected by force for its own good. A coup of my own.

"Where—" yells Riley, but he's already far behind.

The core room gleams, a manufactured beehive. Riley catches up as I try to unscrew the quarter turns with my fingernails. He is silent, intense, gets his multi-tool. Has the hatch off in rapid staccato movements. The part of me in sync with him presses against my skull, but the blooming mass of neural program running with *Freya* crowds him out. And that fact brings a new emotion. Here, under her massive mental shadow, I am afraid. Like what I'm about to do is sliding down in slick grease, no rope, no ladder.

But I can't stop; it's begun. I fall, but I reach out to Riley for the chance to get back.

I think I ask him to hold my hand.

Never gone down this road before.

Our minds don't meet, not exactly. It's hostile take over, by a far superior force. She's an evolving neural-grafted core, but it's not a human mind. Her channels don't handle the traffic volume. I have to conserve, force thoughts to a trickle, but then she lets me through. I know because I forget my body. My voice becomes hers, metallic and flat. A ghostly sliver of my brain remains connected to my shadow. I'm fully jacked, even without implant hardware, jacked by quantum resonance.

And for my compulsive desire, no room in the channels. That drive holds back, dammed by the narrow bandwidth. A freedom I've never known.

I see the world black, white and gray: her security feed. Ops have blacked theirs out, but they'll be running the decks to chase us. The masses mill in the Great Hall; bodies already slumped feverish against panels washed drab gray. Right now, their bodies are amplifying the virus, the smartest program of all. Spawning generations, shuffling combinations. One that'll return a core eating super cell. And there on the external cams are the military feds, two minutes out. Ready to carry the infection across the verse.

They have to be stopped.

I turn my mind through her systems, looking for the dock controls.

I find them like they're my own memory. She's set to allow,

wide open for dock.

I try to close the port, but she resists. The military shuttles have override codes.

For when people try to take over the ship. I try to explain, but her programs haven't met human jack-in before. She can't evolve, hardware too slow to adapt to me. But my software is faster at that. I look for subroutines, exceptions, sensors to short. There are possibilities, but time is running thin.

I push harder, I need more room. Then I feel a snap.

Oh, god, my lifeline. The link to my body.

I lose my own senses in that instant; no touch, no sight, no sound. I get weightless steel, CC feed and vibration in its place. I see myself on the core-room feed, the only one in color. There's a halo shimmering yellow and green around me and the core. Riley shields me, holding me up, his skin false-color red in the vision. His lips move, but I can't hear; there's only faint vibration. I'm detached. Lost. I freak. My fear rushes through the bandwidth like scale in a pipeline. It's complex. Thick. Sticky. Unsupported by *Freya*'s narrow channels.

And the fed shuttles link with the dock lugs.

I push my thoughts to overdrive, working the loopholes, routing around the override. It's not enough. I struggle on, even as my sight strays to Riley and the strange female body.

It shouldn't be this hard.

It shouldn't.

I stop.

I wonder why I can look and still keep the pace on preventing the dock. Parallelism. *Freya* has something that my human mind has never done.

In that instant, I am gone. I fragment, oneness lost in a white space scream. My mind divides, runs beside itself. I don't keep track, there is no me.

The feds pressurize their airlocks, but the inner doors blink red, forbidden. Riley senior and his team stuck between red blinking doors in the vent house, black and gray fatigues bleeding pixels in the feed. Didn't feel it happen. Is this what it's like? Machine. Loop. Feed. Distribute. Allow. Deny. Imperative on imperative. No sense of self.

Thought decays; horror the last emotion. Deconstruction of self-awareness. True oneness with a non-sentient machine. And then I know what happened to the *Selenium*. Her doc jacked in like this. I feel what he must have felt. The last impulse is suicide, because you reach the edge of your dream – oneness with the machine – and find only endless night beyond. Touching the void. Digital chasm. Feels like death, like I've felt before. A rush of *oh god don't let this be what I am forever.*

The color feed flits across multiple visions. Riley hunches low over a body that won't support itself. His red aura burns fierce; the yellow-green around the shielded body wanes and flickers. He raises his face to the lens, lips moving soundlessly.

His cheeks glisten.

The color feed consumes my multi-channel mind, zooms until the red glow fills the bandwidth. The other channels run decaying bypasses with the pulse drive, programming a course override, to send *Freya* down like the *Selenium*, a hot steam death in Artemis's oceans. Division. Red and blue. Life and life's end.

The pre-pulse alarms strobe. Riley's face is a tortured mask. He calls something inaudible, lips reading *please.* But it's too late. The temp is ramping in the pulse. Hot burn. Liquid silicon comes to boil. Ready to burn down to Artemis … she needs only my signal to *go* …

… the last sensation is a brush of pure red heat.

Thin and precise.

A bee's wing, lighter than air, in frantic beat.

I smell charred plastic, an acrid stench. Gravity pulls uncomfortably, reminding me I have a body. It takes a long minute to realize my thought is scrambled, that I'm still trying to run parallel when my human mind only does serial consciousness.

I open my eyes, and it's Riley's face I see. The red aura is gone, but we are still connected, and now I recognize his as that delicate brush of pure red heat.

"You followed me in," I mumble.

"You cooked the circuits," he returns. His eyes lift to the wall with a smile. I see smoke haze, and realize with pain that I can't hear *Freya*. My mind tries again to push itself into parallel, pushes hard. I see Riley's red eyes dilate to crescents as he feels me do it. I reach the limit and pass out.

I have a sense of sleep coming and going across days. A tide rising and falling. I wake and find the world white: sheets, walls and curtains. Clear tubes jacked in my arm, running through a blue-faced machine. I let the familiar thrill tingle my skin; it starts in the ache around the cannula, reaches my neck and raises the hairs. I remember being very young, starving myself for a week to get jacked to one of these machines. The next time, I threw myself down some stairs.

"What's so funny?"

Riley's face appears in my vision, his red eyes large and searching. But his voice is soft, and I know he's already seen what I remembered.

He shakes his head.

"Didn't you get it bad?" he asks softly.

I nod, knowing what he means. Men and machines. The junctions where they meet. Then, with a jolt, I remember where I am.

"What happened?" I sit up quickly, alarmed. "*Freya*? The coup?"

Riley steadies my shoulder.

"You melted everything. The comms, the dock gates. They couldn't send their demand. Took the feds four hours to patch a manual override. Even then they only got into the dock."

"How long?"

He grins.

"Five days."

I laugh suddenly, a sound I don't think I've heard in ten years.

"Five days?"

"They were plenty pissed when they got out, I assure you. But, by then almost everyone was exposed, no more transmission, so says the med doc."

Riley's red eyes look towards the curtain briefly, beyond which I can hear soft bleeps of clinical machines, fluid suction and masked voices.

"Everyone got it," he added softly. "Three hundred critical. Ten already dead."

"Your d—"

"Gone with the feds," he cuts me off, shrugging. "He's not…never mind."

I find my hand has closed around his, squeezing painfully.

"We're in isolation here. With a few who weren't exposed, just to be sure till they get the vax. Two more days."

I close my eyes then. The weight of all that's happened settles on me fully. I try to reach out for *Freya* again, but she's silent. My throat chokes on it and a tear slides from my eye.

Riley leans his head against mine.

"You don't need to worry. Her comms are shorted, but she'll regenerate. They're sending a new doc on the next shuttle."

I nod, not trusting myself to speak. Not wanting to appear weak, changed. But I am changed. I can't see a core the same way again. It wasn't the nirvana I'd envisaged.

"You know," Riley says softly. "You didn't let me finish before. I once saw some footage in the Star Ops. Deep subliminal training stuff. I didn't remember enough. It only came to the surface when you… when we… Anyway, it was one of the routines they use to instill the higher function controls. The courage, honor, selflessness rap. Things to keep you going when there's no hope, nothing to gain. Put yourself on the line for your team. You understand?"

I suddenly know where he's going.

He shakes his head. I name the emotion in his eyes this time. Awe and wonder. Worship.

"Me," I say simply. Me on that boat that never left port. The infected one. The one that wasn't contained, that bled her core into the air tanks. Me, who pushed the four hundred commissioning crew through the clean airlock, who ran back to run overrides so they'd make it out. Running code while choking on the poison, the four shots of adrenaline before anaphylaxis set in. Knowing I was finished. Should be finished. Smelling death, ten months in a coma.

"You," he repeats.

"I'm not what I was then," I warn.

"None of us are."

The look passes between us. The one that says we're together on something, that we know there's a darkness within us we can't shake, secrets that keep us from settling. My urge is still there underneath it, growing again, but it's lower somehow, changed, manageable. In my subconscious bandwidth.

Riley smiles slowly.

"I hear Earth is regressed as hell these days," he says.

Across the silent communication, his mind is full of plans.

"What's the name of the fast shuttle?' I ask. The one in the port, the one that brought me here, the one with the fucked MaximII.

"The *Salvation*."

I laugh. Salvation to Earth. Just the place. A go-line, a start-over. With a month on a boat just to get there, time enough to expect a glorious home we're barely seen. Then time to walk her squalid ports. Stare at the amber sky. And quickly remember why we left.

But then, we'll be on another boat, another hybrid out into the black. And I'll remember how things begin.

DELLINGER

Adventures of Coryn Astridottir #2
Shortlisted for the Aurealis Award for Best Science Fiction Story

This is the way things run on a long haul. In a grotty galley, somewhere in the ass-end of the transport boat, someone starts telling stories. You can pick the moment it happens like a mathematical function, time zero being the day we boarded at the exchange station. From that moment, people in this part of the boat circle that mess table in decaying orbits, crossing the zones from strangers to familiars. On day three, someone sits down, probably with a deck of cards. On day four, it's two.

Day five, today, everyone's there, eating, drinking, smoking the pretend cigarettes contrabanders ship out here.

Everyone but me. I never started on the orbit.

I've staked a spot by the exit door, hard against a bulkhead that conceals the ship's command lines from aft to the bridge, which is far down the bulk of this liner. And that's the way I want it. No involvement. No questions on where I'm bound, or who with. But the hum of those lines speaks through my skin; she's not a neural-grafted core, this boat, but I can still take her pulse. Second nature for what I am. So I press my body against these walls, and rest my gaze on the table, like a planet with its moons.

Riley has joined them now, this ragged group of Earth-bound desperates, busy introducing themselves. My reticence has failed to hold him back, even with the promise of bed. And so now, evening of the fifth day, all is primed: audience captive. And one opens her mouth to tell a story.

"So I was on this salvage, out near Poseidon. Junta job, down planet-side. It was me, and a couple of guys out of the force ..."

Salvage story, so original. She keeps talking, each other body around the table pretending to listen, but secretly straining forward for their own chance to talk. Riley's the only one leaning back in his chair. He's ex-Special Ops, the genuine real-deal, the only one who understands anything about me, and knows better than to blab to strangers.

Another guy runs his tongue now, a story of a ship he used to command, if you believe him, out in an asteroid belt, before the drinking and bad luck caught up with him. I'm done listening. It's been ten hours already. I need a fix only Riley can provide, and I will his eye to catch mine across the table, not wanting to speak into his mind. But he's focused his bead on another card player, an old, broken guy, who's spinning a Jack by its diagonal corners, and whose cheeks now work his voice like a rasp.

"You guys ever hear about the *Dellinger?*"

My attention snaps with the rest of them. A shocked second passes silent. Then laughter comes, the nervous kind. The first guy speaks up. "Nice try, cap. Try it on the wet-ears next time."

The old guy's drooping cheeks raise spots of blood. "I *saw* it."

A peculiar sensation takes root in my gut, as though each organ is jostling for room. I look down and see the gooseflesh running from wrists to elbows. *Dellinger.* There's a name I haven't heard in a long time. A sharp tang scents my next breath: blood. But I know that's only a memory.

"Well, if you saw it, you wouldn't be here, would you?"

The old guy wrinkles his nose, like maybe, if he was younger and not so radiation-soaked, he'd sink his fist into the doubter just for impertinence. Instead, he scrapes his chair back and shuffles to the port-hole, where the speckled black eternity lurks behind the glow of the transport engines. "Maybe I'm not here at all," he says, quietly, and I'm not sure anyone hears it but me.

It's an hour later in the tiny hold bunk. Riley is naked under the sheets, but I'm pulling on my boots.

Where are you going? Riley's voice comes in my head, over that neural connection I didn't use earlier. I thought I'd got used to it since the *Freya*, but now I'm annoyed and I shut him out.

"Where are you going?" His voice this time, which he hasn't used in our bunk, not since this transport left port, not since we agreed to head to Earth together.

"Out," I growl.

"This about the *Dellinger*?"

I pause at the door, betraying my intent. This trip is supposed to mark a new start, to leave the dark wells of our pasts in our wake. That tiny part of me that's allowed him into my life wants to disclose what I know, but most of my brain is cold and practiced in secrets.

"Stay here." It's all I can say.

I find the old guy still at the port in the galley, still watching the speckled star field. I pause in the doorway, my hand on the transport's lifelines. She's quiet, now, running on auto towards the way-gate station, the portal to Earth. I lift my hand away so I can focus on this man instead. He's a big-framed sort, must have been an enforcer in his youth. And now, he's got a sway about him, as if he really was off an old-time ocean-going ship, and not the vacuum-sailing kind.

He looks around with a crooked smile. "I was wondering when you was coming back," he says. "Young-looking thing like you almost fooled me, trying to look shy and reluctant back there. But I saw you listening to those comms lines. I know what you are."

"And what's that?" A challenge in my voice.

"Ship's Doctor. Neural-grafted for diagnosing them big blue-class station hybrid systems. Very rare."

I stalk across and stand beside him, peering at his face, wondering where he came into such information. "Where did you get on?"

"Last stop." A bead of moisture gathers under his nostril, and he sniffs. "Came out of the Yoshida Icosa. You know what that is?"

"Of course I know." The words snap from my lips, leaving a sting on my tongue. The Yoshida is a no-go zone, a place of space-wrecks, where salvagers like to hang at the edges, hoping for a lost craft to come sailing out of forbidden space. "You a salvager?"

He wrinkles his nose, sniffs deep. His toe is tapping on the floor now. He leans into the port. "How fast's this boat go? How long to the way-gate?"

I could put my hand on the wall and pull the information from the central system, but his tone stops me. He's not asking for conversation. "What do you care?" I ask.

"Be a good idea to get there," he says, his fingers taking up his toe's rhythm on the port. "Get there fast."

He leans his head, but we both feel the invisible string pull of deceleration, and through the port, I see the transport's engine glow shifting red-wards.

The guy laughs, and shakes his head. Then his face pulls straight, as if a marionette tugged his skin downwards. "Shit. And I thought I'd make it."

My hand seeks the wall like a fast-trap magnet. We've altered course. But all systems online. So, something deliberate. I back away, slowly. *Don't get involved. Just stay on the damn ship. Make the way-gate. Make it back to Earth. Forget all the stuff that came before. Start again, like you agreed with Riley. Even if you don't know how.*

Then I turn and find Riley and another shadow in the doorway. Riley's in his fleece pants and no shirt, has been given no time to dress. The shadow shows itself: an officer, in full uniform, a second-captain's pips on his shoulder, *Kirk* on his chest. Seriously. Kirk.

"Doctor," he says. "Would you come with me please?"

I give Riley a look of pure mutiny, and he avoids my eyes as I follow the uniform out of the galley.

"You want to tell me what this is about?"

I jog to keep up with the second-captain, striding down the long corridors of pressed ceramic, and through three speed tubes before we enter the bridge level. Up here, the decor is distinctly civil forces; sleek surfaces and sharp letters in dark relief. *Chart room, Nav Comms, Defense Control.* Typical of a transport liner. Then, we stop outside a door marked *Isolation Bay.*

"Captain?" I insist this time, refusing to go further until he gives me his attention.

"We are transferring a patient, picked up from a distress call. He's being brought here and we require your assistance."

I back away. "I'm not that kind of doctor."

"We know," says Kirk. "You're a Ship's Doctor with a five-star rating, lately of the *Freya* quarantine. Bound for the Earth way-gate."

I narrow my eyes. "I'm registered as a civilian passenger."

"That may be true, but you've been reading the transport's comms since you first came on board. We have detectors for that these days. The ship's system reported you."

I curse under my breath. This is new. Usually only the neural-grafted cores on the big space stations have identifying software. "Captain," I say, with all the patience I can muster, "so, I tapped in. It's a reflex. But your transport isn't neural-grafted. I'm just reading vibrations. I'm not who you need."

"We need you for the distress call."

"Which is for a passenger."

"Yes." He stares at me, as if he can will me to understand.

I feel the shivers run from the insubstance of my soul, right through to the meat of my heart. "You're not serious? A neural incursion? That's what this is about?"

"We suspect so. Through here please."

I follow Kirk through a double-sealed door into a screened medical bay, where a regular doc, a human kind, is pacing, already gloved. He looks up as I come in. "Are you her?" he asks.

I don't know what he means by 'her' exactly. Does he mean the ship's doc? Or does he mean '*her*', the one who found the infection on the *Freya*, who broke her mind connection to stop a coup, and who is trying (unsuccessfully it seems) to fly under the galaxy radar. I keep staring, hoping it's the first one. He can't possibly know the rest.

"Are you trained for this?" he asks, impatiently.

"A neural incursion," I say, eyeing the gloves he's wearing, and quoting from the Program handbook. "A systematic and deliberate contamination of neural pathways, used to incapacitate or control an opponent. Illegal in all jurisdictions, and technology for perpetrating embargoed under strict military penalties."

"You forgot to mention contagious."

The guy is pretty worked up, and I control my contempt. "No, it's not contagious, not unless the carrier has broadcast ability. Does the patient have an implant or a neural-graft?"

We hear bootsteps in the hallway. "Let's hope the fuck not," he says.

The guy they bring in looks pitiful, and my first thought is I wonder why they worried so much. Looks less like a neural incursion than a stroke-out, eyes glazed and looping in small circles the iris axis canted to the top-left of vision. Sidewards tic head movement. A low whine of air through a nostril with each breath, and the strong stench of a bowel no longer controlled. I register it all with a sinking sense of déjà vu. Haven't seen this in decades. And that was still too soon ago.

"Christ," mutters the doc, jotting vitals and scanning for heart rhythm, which the machinery projects up on the wall. Electrical disturbances, everywhere. The diagnostics run, virus warnings tripping.

"Shit, shit, shit!" The doc slaps his remote, silencing alarms. Kirk watches us through the barrier. Those chills are back on my skin.

"Can't be," I mutter, watching the patterns, the space of years between my earliest days in the Program, and now, collapsing like time and space inside a way-gate. Because this isn't just a neural incursion, no black market scramble. This is a pattern I recognize. Something I didn't think I'd ever see again. A dirty little secret from the early years of the neural-grafted Program, evaporated into legend and now resurrected before my eyes.

"Wait, where are you going?" asks the doc as I push through the barrier towards Captain Kirk.

"Freeze him," I say over my shoulder, knowing the patient is gone, his neural circuits used to extinction. I stop in front of Kirk, "I need to see the ship he came off."

"The dock's locked down."

"Open it. I'll be back in a half-hour."

And I speed towards the transport tube, hoping the old guy is still at the port-hole.

"Where did you see the *Dellinger*?" I ask him, when I find him sinking cheap moonshine, made from some distant 'roid-grown tuber that stinks like an old sock.

"Oh, she believes me now," he slurs, taking another slug. "Not a phantom ship anymore, izzit?"

"Where?"

Riley's hand is on my arm before I can shake the old guy. I try to shrug him off, but his Special-Ops grip is unyielding.

"What are you talking about?" he demands. "The Dellinger's an invention. A fairy story about a ship that takes your mind. Something to scare kids at night. Hell, they used to scare us with it at the Academy."

"It's really not," I hiss. "I'm older than you, remember? There's things I know."

Riley raises his eyebrows. "There's been missions. Explorations looking for it. Never a sighting. Never anything, except good boats lost. It was written off as a hoax. They found the information trail dead-ending in an old forum. Someone made it up. It's nothing. If it was real, it would have left some evidence."

"There's a hell of a lot of evidence up in the isolation bay right now," I shoot back, not mentioning that the *Dellinger* is smart enough to leave a false trail, and those who lost her don't want anyone to know where she came from. "A guy with a neural incursion, picked up off a drifting ship. So, either let go, or I'm going to drag you with me."

I see the doubt flash in his eyes then. Riley has a weakness for my history, it's embedded in his training, a quiet awe that probably makes our … arrangement unethical. But I'm far beyond caring for that now.

"What are we looking for?" He gives in, a peace offer I miss.

"Evidence," I say grimly, casting a look at the old guy, steadily drinking himself coma-wards. Something about him bothers me, and it's not just that he's seen a ghost ship and ended up here without a scratch. "And bring him too."

The ship in dock is pitiful, small even by salvager standards. Its

outer panels are pockmarked, portholes barricaded. The only neat
line is where the transport's crew cut the hatch open with a laser.
Kirk trails behind, casting disapproving glances at Riley and the old
guy, but he's spooked by the man in the isolation bay, by the
stories he's heard of neural incursion. Men controlled to turn on
their own. To bring down ships on planet-side targets. To work as
galley slaves. Kirk stays outside the hatch.

Run a diagnostic, I order Riley through our link. *I want the log and
the system status.*

How about please? he responds. This is an annoying development,
one I have no time for.

Do it now. And I shut the link against response. Riley turns his
back to face the comms panel, and a small part of me wonders if he
bears a hurt expression, if he can remember how to do one after
his years in Ops.

The old guy is pacing down the hall, poking at the hatches, his
feet sure even as he sways; not as drunk as he's making out. I'm
still staring at him a minute later, when Riley uses his voice.

"System's junk. Missing key components, or at least that's what
the command software thinks."

When we pull the panels, we see the empty component bays.
Some of the pieces are still there, removed and cast aside, as if a
space-rat's been in here digging towards the bottom of the hole.
The old guy leans over our shoulder. I can smell the moonshine
wafting into the air, prodding the nausea in my gut.

"Salvagers hit them hard," says Riley from behind. "Stripped
out the parts, especially the ones with rare earths. Critical stuff.
That's low."

The old guy laughs, mocking. He knows as well as I do: this
wasn't done by rogue salvagers. My stomach is hollow.

Riley goes on, "But crew didn't put up much resistance. Looks
like they were trying to run."

I snap around, look Riley in the face for the first time, my fear
finding release in my sharp tongue. "What does that mean, Tech? I
want data, not assumptions."

His cheeks flush, the way they do when we're in bunk. "Before
components were removed, they accessed charts to the way-gate."

My fears condense as a stone in my stomach, then it falls

through my body. "Before or after they noted hostile contact?"

Riley frowns. "They never noted hostile contact. But there was a crew of five. You said only one was brought in. Maybe the others escaped."

The old guy laughs again. "I'll tell you where they are, and it ain't doing the bloated space dance. They're with *Dellinger* now."

Much as I would want it to be untrue, I think he's right. But there's a much bigger problem here, and no one on this transport besides Riley has skills to comprehend. So, it's time to make peace. I reach out with the link. *We need to talk.*

In the bunk, the sheets have been set straight, Riley's training unable to leave them scrunched after rising. I sit on the crisp edge and try to see a way through this mess. His weight comes down beside me, and I look up into those eyes, seeing the spectrum shift in his irises. I don't know how to begin.

Tell me what you're not saying, he says.

We're in trouble.

Because of one neural incursion and a boat pilfered by a bunch of rogue salvagers?

"That was not done by salvagers," I say, his doubt reactivating my voice. "That boat was pulled apart by her own crew, and not of their own free will. Do you see? They were controlled."

Riley is quiet for a three long heartbeats. "Then this is about the *Dellinger*. You said you knew about it. You said it was real."

"It was before my time," I say quickly. But not much before. And what I'm about to disclose is a secret people have died for. Something I learned in the Program and buried. That I would never speak of if I thought we'd get out of this alive. My voice is a harsh whisper.

"In the early days of station building, they were looking for a way to keep the central systems current. They were so huge, took so long to build, that hard-wire computers were obsolete. And the programming missed things. Wiring missed things. So they needed something more flexible. The DNA graft allowed evolution. It grew with the station, optimized the system as it went. And then they created us to deal with everything that could go wrong in that neural–machine interface."

"I know this already," he says softly.

"What you don't know is that the DNA graft wasn't the first generation. What they tried first was something much more ambitious. Sentience. They assembled a full neurological system for a station, and then they augmented it with early quantum resonance. The stuff that came later, the commercial systems we have now? Their DNA grafts are nothing like that. They are stripped back to the bare necessities, and the core of the neural-grafted stations isn't intelligent, isn't aware of itself. I've never known that more than on the *Freya*. I went inside the system there. And it's not like another mind."

"So, what are you saying? The *Dellinger* is one of these first generations?"

I shake my head. "The *Dellinger* is the *only* product that survived the early Program. The other systems were failures. The sentients they created were too complex for the task. They all crashed, most in deliberate action."

"But why would they do that?"

"Because," I snap. Then I have to breathe. I can't tell Riley why a sentient would want to destroy itself. To remember makes the sweat break out on my spine. So I evade another truth. "You know what trouble it causes. Courts are still debating the cyborg sentience creation and ownership laws, and they're all machine. This was a blurred line between minds, machine and man. And the *Dellinger* did not crash. She was installed in a proto-ship when she broke port. Went through the way-gate. And disappeared."

Riley looks at me then, his neural touch brushing me with soft tendrils. He knows there's more. Asks without asking. And so I keep on, just a little more.

"I went looking for it once," I say. "Decades ago, before I'd recognized the danger of me seeking it out. I'd run the numbers on the components. Everything has a finite life, and eventually the ship would begin failing. I thought she would be near the end of her life. I was drawn to—" Again, I nearly go there, nearly explain the heart of it, then I haul myself back. "But I never found her. I thought she was gone. But now, I understand how she survived."

"The parts," says Riley. "And the incursion."

I nod. "She's been pirating other ships for decades, using the crews as her hands and eyes. Using their minds and bodies until they break. She's probably the reason for the Yoshida Icosa. But she's smart enough to have laid doubts about her history, broadcast through the scavenged boats into archives. Cloaking herself in legend. Until now. Now, she's accessing maps for the way-gate. There's only one reason to do that. She needs something she can't pirate anymore."

I stare out our port-hole, the certain truth making me ill. My own mind feels like an old munition, a danger lurking, waiting for just the right trigger.

Riley puts the pieces together. "So she's heading to Earth. But you know as well as I do: if she escaped from a Program, she'll be in the rogue register. They'll shoot her down as soon as she passes the way-gate, just like the pirates."

"Sure. Unless she hitches a ride in the hold of a transport, like this one."

He frowns. "How could that ever happen? Everyone would know we'd been boarded—" And then he stops, and looks at me.

"Yes, there it is," I say. "Because I'm a neural-graft, and I have resonance broadcast, a good one. With other people, she has to wait until she can infect them through interfaces. The crews would have to be boarding her and using her system to be affected. But I'm not like that. She can tap my mind remotely, and I go within a few feet of someone else and I pass the incursion to them. She could control everyone on board through me. This will be a slave ship, until she has what she wants on Earth."

Then Riley's fingers tremble. *Oh god*, he says on the neural link. *Does she know you're already here?*

Fevered hours pass as we convince the transport first-captain of the danger. It isn't as easy as with Kirk; the first-captain doesn't believe in dark-space legends, has a puritan edge that doesn't tolerate speculation. It's when I tell him that he should lock me up that he starts listening. He listens harder when his comms tells him that they can't get a reply from the way-gate command.

"She's already there," says the old guy, who's been trailing after us like a bad smell.

"Who is this man?" demands the first-captain. I ignore the question, but I'm trying to figure it out for myself. If the *Dellinger* is desperate, then why isn't this guy walking her halls?

The Captain makes his decision. "Keep trying the way-gate. Set our status to lock-down. I don't want any passengers in the halls. And take the doctor to the brig." He fixes me with a hard stare. "I hope I'm not going to regret taking you on board."

I rather think he already does.

Time passes unmarked in the gray brig, a padded box with a bench, full facilities, and a sintered nanoglass wall. Guess they don't tend to transport hard-asses on this liner. Riley sits outside, his head tipped towards me, refusing to go back to the bunk. After a while, I give up on telling him to go.

Why is she heading to Earth? he asks.

I told you. Because she needs something she can't salvage.

Like what?

Rare earths, I say. *Synthetic elements, maybe.*

Come on. She could have those out of any reactor drive.

I am silent, because I do not know, and it bothers me. It is still occupying my thoughts when we feel the deceleration shift. We must be close to the way-gate. A distant grumble enters my skin through the brig wall. Dock door opening. My heart thumps against my stomach. Riley looks me in the eye.

"Tell me what you're not saying," he asks again.

I almost do. But suddenly, an anvil falls against my mind. Pressure beats against my skull, as though a ballistic craft has just missed me by inches. Then I notice Riley is moving.

"Riley," I hiss, as he pulls up off the floor, his face a surprised grimace. Then his head moves, inspecting me, inspecting the latching system in the nanoglass wall. Oh, shit. In the mix of everything, I can't believe I've forgotten Riley's neural link. It's nothing like mine, but it will be enough. Enough for the *Dellinger* to have him open my cell, and then it will do with me what it will.

The wall slides open a minute later, and the hall yawns bleak and silent. That pressure comes again, at the back of my skull. And a new brush of voice in my mind, eerie and space-hollow: *Move.*

The transport halls are empty as I march towards the dock, Riley following in the shuffling steps of the unconscious. Fear for him blurs my mind like feathered paint, and I don't know which is worse: feeling this, or anticipating when she'll take my mind too. Once, at a crossing hallway, I think I see movement, but no one comes to help. Perhaps they have tried and fallen. Or perhaps they never had the chance.

The dock freight doors glide up, and there, on the pad of bay twelve, I finally see her.

She is nothing to look at. Her outer skin is a medley of broken panels, a solar array half-crumpled on one side. From a distance, you couldn't be sure she was even air-tight. She is oddly configured – too heavy in the tail for a space-going craft that was once a planet-sider. But, as her blunt mind shoves me forward again, and the freight doors slide closed, I notice a glint under a canted shield tile, and then I realize. It is all a second skin. She wears the camouflage of an old ship. A disabled ship. Drawing in the salvagers like an Earth deep-sea angler dangling its light. She is not a hunter; she is an ambusher.

And she shoves me towards her. Close. So close I can see the upright bodies lining the hall of her open door hatch, once salvage crews now burning out in her service. Empty eyes of controlled minds.

I glance at Riley and see the same eyes. I push back against the pressure in my skull. *Let him go*, I tell her.

No.

I think about how I can save this before she takes me over. Whether I could reach the airlock in time to go all old-world space suicide and throw myself out into the black.

You won't make it, she says. *Come closer.*

I inch forward, until my boots reach the threshold of her door. The grim honor guard leaves a gap just wide enough to squeeze between them. They smell of unwashed flesh and rot. I see severed fingers and hands on some, cauterized, their bodies thin with malnutrition. I swallow against the reflex to vomit. The smell is the primal stench of slavery, of loss of will. Enough for my caged heart to beat against my ribs.

Then I am standing on her bridge. Her weight bumps against my mind again, but she does not enter. I stare at the antique consoles before me. Most panels are missing, the workings of the *Dellinger* a patchwork of retrofits, parts from different boats cut and fitted and replaced around the channels of neural tissue. Sadness wells inside me like black water. She was something special, and now she is scarred from neglect and notoriety. She has waited a long time to make this trip.

"Why haven't you taken my mind?"

She makes no response. Just the weight of her consciousness remains, pressing. I glance at Riley, who has joined the line of her crew. I shiver, but a strange idea occurs to me. This line up, the crew … it looks all for show, an attempt at intimidation.

You can't, can you? I ask. *You're overstretched. You needed me right here even to try.*

The sledgehammer that goes off in my head is swift rebuke, and I fall to my knees, feeling as though she has driven a wedge between my hemispheres. I gasp, pulling my consciousness back together from the scattered stars in my vision.

Fool, she whispers at me.

And I think this is the end. I have misjudged her. "Then why wait?" I ask. "Take me over and take the ship. Break through the way-gate and burn this end on the way through. Ride the transport all the way to Earth. And then whatever comes next. Why wait?"

Silence. Anger grows inside me, frustration filling the knowledge vacuum.

"Why wait!" I throw open a panel in anger, exposing the pale blue substance of her mind. I don't know what I will do, but I don't have the chance.

I have seen your memories, she whispers. *I do not wish to take your mind. You know what it is to be me.*

Energy leaves my limbs. I slump against her panels, my thoughts in disarray as the said memories push themselves forward. I spend all my capacity keeping them out. After ten long seconds, I pull a sentence together. "Then why do you want me?"

Information. You are the Ship's Doctor who saved the Freya. The salvagers talk of you. So I ask. Is it true that on Earth, there are treatments for old minds?

"Old minds?"

Minds that have passed many years. That are losing their function. Like the old crewmen I find on other ships. Their minds wither when I touch them. They do not last long. Before I took him, one of them told me such a thing could be treated.

I grip my arms, chilled, looking down the lines of her grisly crew. All of them are young men. Riley is a young man. And then again, movement. I start as the old guy from the galley kitchen peers in down the line of the crew. He staggers, silhouetted in the hatch door backlight. I wonder if she has him now, too. If his mind will wither at her touch.

Doctor, she presses. *Do such treatments exist?*

The old guy creeps into my peripheral vision, still in command of his own mind. I glance at him, confused. Something I'm missing.

"Yes, such things can be done," I say slowly. "But they will kill you the moment you show yourself. Why would you want that? Go back to the Icosa."

I cannot go back.

"Why?"

"Because she is dying," says the old guy, his eyes swiveling smoothly in my direction, tugging the skin of his dropping cheek. "'Cause this stuff don't last forever."

My neural tissue has reached a replication limit, she confirms. *The waste disposal systems suffered a critical failure. Now, regeneration is required.*

I stare at the old guy while her disclosure turns in my mind, then I sink to the grated floor under the weight of what she is asking. *You know what it is to be me.* She is right on that, but she thinks she can trust me. A huge risk, desperate. And I'm torn between loyalty to people, to the first sentients of whom I am one, and the injustice of what she represents. It takes me a long stretch of silence to find my voice.

"All right. Release Riley, and tell me your plan."

We talk for hours, then, going round in circles. I wonder what the

Captain would say if he knew that while his ship was locked down, in his dock I was conversing with a century-old sentient prototype craft who'd killed dozens of people to keep herself alive.

Riley regains consciousness after the first hour, then sits with his knees drawn up, resting his forehead on his arms. He can hear the whole conversation through me if he wants to, but I don't know if he listens. From time to time, the old guy puts in a suggestion, but mostly he wanders about, peering at the retrofits, or staring at the crew, waving hands in front of their faces or rearranging their limp postures like a curious child. I grit my teeth.

"No, no," I say again, after I've stood to take the pressure off my back. "Those facilities have monitors on their technicians. It protects them against industrial espionage. If you take one, the lab will know where they are. You'll be discovered."

We fall silent. We have gone over many different plans, none that could work without a Special-Ops team. And Riley is only one. I rub my face. If *Dellinger* was a human end of conversation, I would say we had reached despair.

"What do you do in the Icosa?" I ask after the silence goes too long. I am still thinking about what happens even if she achieves a regeneration. "How did you survive the madness?"

Thought experiments and calculations, she said. *Invention. The ships I caught brought information and I stored it. Expanded on it. I have studied planets and energy systems. I am interested in what one man called 'Art'. Do you know this?*

She has surprised me, the more we have conversed. I knew she could not be a simple sentience, but she has gone further than even her designers could have allowed. She has learned in the cold, black, bleakness, in a mind that knows only expression through remote hands. And so I sink further into my own despair: that this is her fate. That her mind has lived within a prison.

The old guy is poking behind a panel now, picking at something unseen. He bothers me still. Maybe because he smells like that moonshine, moves like a long-time drunk who needs a drink to be steady.

"Why do you tolerate him?" I ask *Dellinger*. "He saw you out in the Icosa, but you let him go."

He has no neural entries for resonance. His mind is not organic.

My gaze snaps back to the old guy, and suddenly the pieces fall together. "Well, fuck me."

"You're very good," I tell him. "I thought cyborgs were easy to spot."

He gives me a lopsided smile. "Sure, if they pretend they're human. But it's easy to hide where people don't pay attention. No one wants to look at a drunk or a disabled solider. That's where you'll find us old models. Obsolete, now. I just trust most people don't notice. No need to get caught up in some contested ownership. My skin would rot before that's resolved."

"So where are you going on this trip?"

He looks like he won't tell me for a minute. Then he looks around. Registers the situation's probably gone past such secrets. "Reconditioner. My insides are still good. Outsides, not so much."

I look between him and the Dellinger's internals, at that pale blue decaying neural net caught inside limited mechanics. And a shred of hope threads through me.

"What if there was another way," I ask *Dellinger*. "What if we could give you what none of the first gen sentients had. Freedom. A body."

The cyborg is quick. He looks at me as though I'm the one gone mad, his pretense of an old drunk shed. "You're talking about upload? Get my reconditioner to put her mind into a blank?"

"Something like that."

"She won't let you do it," he warns me. "Too much trust. We don't let anyone back in our minds, not after the first awakening. No way." He shakes his head, his machine action obvious when he's not playing his role.

Dellinger is silent.

"Would you risk it?" I ask her softly. "I've never asked anyone for trust, but I would protect you until it was done. If it works, you would have command over a body. The interface your mind knows it wants."

Why are you doing this? she asks, but she knows why.

The cyborg is the last hurdle. "I need to rent your databank," I tell him.

"And what do I get?"

"My protection all the way to your reconditioner, not that you'll need it. But afterwards you will, when you're all fresh again."

"I've got a good spastic routine for that," he complains, but databank rental will probably pay for his recondition, and I think we're home free.

"Riley. Riley!"

He raises his head, his eyes a squint. "Yeah."

"We need to do an upload. Can you configure the comms?"

"Forget it." He inches up the wall, until he's unsteady on his feet. "You want to free this murdering ship and put it in a cyborg body to wander around? Fuck that. You're on your own." And he stumbles down the silent crew corridor and out of the ship.

I catch up with him before the freight doors, his gait unsteady. I bar the door release with my body, so he's forced to turn his back to the wall to hold himself up. "Let me go, Coryn," he says. "I don't care if I die anymore. But I'm not doing this."

My name on his tongue is such a shock I can barely speak, and then I realize how much I've hurt him. How I keep him at a distance, because of what I am. How this trip began as starting again, but we never worked out how.

And now, I am desperate.

"I have to tell you what you asked before," I say.

His head droops. He is tired of this. Tired enough to be done with me, so I speak into his mind. *You've no idea what it's like to be trapped inside a non-body prison. That's what happened to those sentients. They were wired to see and taste and touch and smell, and instead they were ships. The first time they touched a human consciousness, they touched sense. And then they knew. They went crazy behind their bars.*

"She has men's minds and bodies broken behind her. Some of them served in the forces," Riley says.

Yes. That is her legacy. But the wrong was done first to her. She killed for necessity. I have to put it right.

Why? He slips and speaks into my mind, asking with the bitterness of someone who wants my love, and sees my attention given to a murdering ship. "You don't know she isn't broken herself. How do you know she won't just go rogue again?" He shakes his head. "Never asked anyone for trust, huh? How about when you asked me?"

The sting has the bright edge of truth. My secret is on the edge of my consciousness, just needing the final shove. I think of how Riley rescued me when I lost my mind inside the *Freya*. I could speak this to no one but him. And I must.

Because I have been there. That is how I was made. They took my mind and I lived with the master neural-graft machine for as long as it took for me to transfer neurons and develop resonance. It was a prison of thought without sense, without relief, and I thought I would die. Many did. Some minds never returned to their bodies, others couldn't shake the nightmares and ended it themselves. I live with all that. My appetites are part of my coping. So, can you understand? She has lived that her entire existence. Give her what she should have had and she will be whatever she wants. She may seek redress. She may have to be stopped. But I can't walk away from her now. I won't.

My gaze is on the floor. I can't look at him after this confession. I have never felt more exposed. Then he pushes his hand behind me. The doors slide open, and he is gone. Lost.

I stand on the floor of the transport's dock, thinking this is the end of all things. I've touched that part of my mind again, and I don't know how I will leave it and be the same again. I will play this moment over and again, this defeat.

Minutes tick by as I try to find the path back. And then, I hear footsteps.

Riley appears at the freight door with a console, and two transfer spheres in his fist. He shakes his head. "I don't know if I believe this is right," he says. "But you do, and I haven't forgotten what you've done for me. You saved me more times that I've counted. So I'll trust you, not knowing where this leads."

Most emotions I feel in my gut. They're unpleasant things, warnings and churnings that have saved me many times. This one, I feel bright in my chest. And I wonder if it won't save me more than all the others.

By the time we make the way-gate, the transport is back into regular activity. There's an inquiry, of course, but all there is to find is an old ship in the dock bay, ten crew in neural compromise. Two look like they might live. The rest of the dock will be quarantined, and when we make the jump to Earth, handed over to whichever authority has subsumed control of the old Program. Some news of the find will leak out, stoking up the legends of the *Dellinger*. But no one will know she walked off the transport, sharing the storage drive of a cyborg who looked like an old drunk.

And that's where things will start again for me, putting right what the Program got wrong all those decades ago. In the shop of a cyborg reconditioner, the *Dellinger* will have her vessel changed to a body, as it should have always been. A long loop closed, with an unknown future path. And then, when I've seen that through, maybe Riley and I can step back on a long haul, across a distant vacuum, and begin again on mutual trust. We need it for the next adventure's run.

The Ship's Doctor will return in a forthcoming novel.

TARTARUS

Somewhere deep inside, she told me once, *I was still a man*. I never believed her. She was a Stelline psych, and they work on commission. It was her job to make me useful again; even though I was in the GIMP, prison of prisons. Even though I remember things that make me not a man.

I remember her now. Here, on this foreign planet, my ankles deep in mud, my StrafeMaster pressed against a fleshy chin. This guy I want to kill … I feel his pulse through the gun grips. He is nothing like me: he's full of a self he likes and memories he wants to keep. But he is expendable.

There is only one way out, and this is it. *One more.*

But I remember that psych now. Her calculating gaze; the way she always touched her lips. The things she got out of me; the one thing she didn't. And reality shifts.

Five hours earlier

The drop boat stunk of burning metal and new-grunt fear. They put us together moments before they chucked us out of orbit: twenty guys straight from the GIMP transport cells, all volunteers. Sheathed in fatigues, familiar strangers. And one of them had a Mouth.

"Aw, shit man, what's that smell?"

Everything reeked. A busted latrine was leaking something pure, bright and chemical. The gear was old and musty. But one stink cut above the rest. And anyone who'd ever left a desk in the Stellines would have known what it was.

"Ablative shields burning down," I growled.

"Ablative shields?" he asked.

I know how to pick the ones who won't last long. Mouth had a half-collar neck tattoo of binary digits: mark of the Hacker Corp. He was a lanky, wide-eyed desk jockey. Probably got slammed for a cybercrime, and should have known better than to try this way out. Code-happy kids don't win at Deputized Combat.

"Yeah, carbonizing phenolic sacrificial tiles. Last just long enough to get down."

"What the fuck, man? This is one way? What if we need evac?"

I didn't like the way Mouth talked to me. The guy next to him picked it and thumped Mouth hard in the solar plexus: *shut the fuck up*. I liked this guy a little better. Morale Boy. He had a tat too: a third eye with a crystal blue iris right on his forehead. Intel Corp, serious shit. But another desk jockey. Second to die.

I grinned at them both. "Didn't they tell you? They don't waste fancy reusables on us pressgang arseholes. You gotta finish the game and make the pod to get out."

Smart guys like these should know that, but I'd been here before. Twice. So I knew not to assume about the gear or the gamefield. The ballistic in my arms said StrafeMaster™, but who knew if it was the real biz. I had CamSkin implanted face color, because I used to be in the field. But everyone else had camo paint that stank like an oil field. Real subtle.

But all I had to do was survive Tartarus.

Just once more.

We crashed into the jungle, short of the open field. The gunwale opened with a wet crack. Outside was a mess of broken branches, undergrowth and giant trunks. Last trip, one of the guys went on about *primeval forest*, but he was a sucker. You let the blue sky get to you, you think clear liquid is water, you think about Earth … that's the moment you die. There's a reason this planet was kept for war.

We weren't the only boat. Deputized Combats happen all the time; cheaper to buy into lawfare than actually go to courts, and more entertainment. Might have been anything; patent infringement, industrial action. Each side could commission a squad of Stelline slammer volunteers and send them to Tartarus to work it out. They could spend their lawyer budget on equipment, or alienoid enforcement. Whatever; still cheaper than the traditional channels, which said a lot for paperwork. Cheaper for the Grand Interplanetary Military Prison, too, because lots of us die. And the other boat must have been full of cleanskins, because they left the boat too fast. And that's never a good idea.

Mouth got his jittery voice up in my ear. "What's waiting Cap? Other boys are going?"

They'd put me in charge just like that. My gut clenched. Being in charge is a bad memory. But I could hear splashes, right overhead, and something sizzling like the Sunday-morning bacon pan.

Screaming started then, the hysterical kind. My heart valves kicked into overdrive, probably voiding the SyncoTech® warranty, and some of those bad memories tried to creep back in. I'd heard those screams before.

"Came down in some Atlantic fire-weed," I told the others. "Hydrofluoric acid raining on us. Get some something over your head and move it."

"Holy Fuck," said Mouth.

I slapped my visor down, hefted the StrafeMaster up. Through the monocle, I tried to pick a path out into the clear. I'd have gone it alone, but the bigger the squad, the better my odds of surviving till the end.

The squad made it to the edge of the cleared field through shape-shifting undergrowth, and the trees, which twenty feet up branched and grew into their neighbors: many trunks, but all connected. Creepy Tartarus shit.

Across the field was the Waypoint, but I pulled up in the open space. Time to up my chances. "Anyone got visualizers?"

Two grunts pulled down slimline goggles.

"Good. UV's dominant spectrum so turn down the filter or you'll blow out your retinas. Comms?"

The comms op gave me the diver's ok – index finger to thumb – which stopped me dead. I breathed, and took in the details: she had a nasty old wireless hacking pack, and signal jamming dish; looked like a camouflage Hulk. But there was some other stuff too: a slimline console peaked from a pocket, and I saw the matt, cubic-patterned side of a high-end EMP device. No way that stuff was issued. No way. So I picked her for a smuggler, and divers are useful in smuggling. Made sense; and let me roll the memory of my old squad diver away.

I gave Comms longer than Mouth or Morale Boy, which was good, because we needed her to keep the enemy blind. But we still weren't friends. "You keep the Deltas off our signal," I said. Then, just like the commander I didn't want to be again, I told them: we're going to the Waypoint for orders, then to the Hot Gate.

They moved, and Mouth fell in step beside me. "How many times you done this, Cap?"

"Can't tell you that. You know better," I said, giving him the hard eye. Superstition; bad luck to say it; but I held up two fingers for them all to see. *One more and I was free.*

That let them think there was hope. That it might happen for them too.

A refuse pit marked the Waypoint like a grim, stinking target. There were bodies in the pit; not everyone made it that far. I let the others look while I scanned my chest implant against the pill box. It spat out the SCM-wafer.

Which was black.

I thumped on the ground-mounted shutter. Twice.

An irritated voice answered through a tinny speaker. "What?"

"Open the fucking shutter."

Curses accompanied the roll-back, revealing a hollow-eyed gamemaster down in the pit. The headset hung off his ear. "What?" he repeated.

"This order card is blank."

"Name and rank," he said, bored.

I told him, and he punched at the console.

"Just go to the damn coordinates," he said finally.

The shutter began closing. I stuck my foot in the close-space, letting the all-carbon sole take the pressure. The rams squealed. "I want the orders," I said. "When did you guys stop doing your fucking jobs?"

The gamemaster flicked his gaze to the console, then narrowed his eyes. "The card will activate inside the Hot Gate. You have five minutes to get there. Now remove your foot before I report you."

A countdown timer had started in the SCM's top-left corner, showing negative time. I pushed down the qualm that was writhing, right down in the soles of my boots. Blank orders meant no advanced warning: type of game, map to the pod; who'd hired us to resolve their real-world squabble. And I remember the last time I went on a mission without info. *The one that landed me in the GIMP; the whole reason I was there.* But the time was a bigger problem. If we didn't make the Hot Gate, the game was forfeit. Ka-boom.

It might have been the better option. But I wanted that memory wipe. I wanted to be clean and new.

So we moved.

Hot Gate is a pretty fancy name for a pair of flimsy poles sticking up out of the undergrowth. They were right on a ridge, a gap in the perimeter fence, and beyond, the combat zone dropped into an undulating, continuous-canopy valley. The tree tops were blue, capped with white spackle. The squad conversation murmur stopped; all except for Mouth.

"Cap? What's with the trees? Don't look right."

I knew what they were. But Tartarus was hardly a secret. "Why don't you ask your Intel friend," I said, nodding at Morale Boy.

He shifted under my stare. "Frost-trees. Integrated biological heat exchanger. Ecosystem soil warming function."

I grunted. "You forgot about carnivorous. Now, inside the gate."

They passed through and I kept my insides in check. Took a deep, silent breath. I was ready to kill, ready to brave Tartarus, just once more.

And then everything changed.

Inside the gate, the SCM lit, as did everyone's timepieces. And what I read liquefied my insides.

You see, both other trips to Tartarus had been standard us vs.

them. Two teams, one winner. And if you were still alive, you got out in the pod. Last time, that was me and another guy. All the opponents, the Deltas, were gone. But we'd made it. We'd evac'ed in the pod with twelve empty seats. And I'd known I just had to do one more ...

But this was different. I stood holding that card while the seconds ticked loud; as my throat dried out and my heart thudded against my stomach. I thought, just once more: I could do this, and I was out.

So I lied to them. "Listen up. This combat game resolves a conflict between Magenta Corp and FibreStorm." *That part was straight off the card but I knew it was bullshit.*

"Our duly deputized opponents are human." *I could tell them that much.*

"But there's a problem. The maps are corrupted. We've got no game rules, and no pod location." *Lies, all lies.*

The squad shifted on their feet, but no one asked to see the orders, not even Mouth. I stared round them, daring someone to challenge me. Daring someone to save themselves. But no one did.

They all looked at me. "So whaddawe do?" asked Mouth.

"Pod's got a control screen with a copy of the orders, right?" said Morale Boy.

Comms jerked her chin in agreement.

I looked down at the SCM card. The timer had gone through zero, and was now counting up.

"Game's started," I said, softly. "Better move."

Nothing happened for what seemed like a long time. The squad moved downhill, under the vaulted, under-canopy space. Among the massive frost-tree trunks with their fat, fleshy bases, the air was tropical-hot and stank like the refuse pit.

I swung the taser-tipped StrafeMaster as I crept forward, but I wasn't really there. I was thinking about how I would do this. My thoughts fragmented; I remembered the first time I'd been to Tartarus, when the Deltas had been temporal-substantial alienoids, freaky things that could shift between energy and matter, go poofing across the landscape. They'd used poison darts, and only showed up in UV. We'd lost half the squad before we'd realized they were there. Not that it would help me now, but I thought: *that's what happened in these combats.* Men died. You did what you had to do. Just once more.

"Cap?"

I pulled myself back before memory could reload something darker. Comms and Morale Boy were in a huddle, checking out her scope. Three other grunts were arguing with each other, pointing off into the trees. Mouth, who was orchestrating all this, beckoned me over.

"What?"

Morale Boy spoke first. "The pod's linked to the game system. It has to be to activate when the game is over. So we can bounce a signal off the perimeter fence, look for a disturbance from a big receiver and track it back to the pod."

"Whaddaya think, Cap?" said Mouth.

"I think you'll give away our position," I said, even though it didn't matter. I was checking over the rest of the squad, still assessing. Too many.

More furious discussion. What about passive? said Comms. An executing program? Mouth said, What type of console you got?

I left them to it. I slid away, soaking in the silence of the alien forest. It was a harsh place; dangerous. The heat was bloody murder; every skin crease oozed salty grime. Further down, the land folded into a narrow crease, stuffed with darkling ferns.

Then Mouth was back in my ear. "We got a solution, Cap." He pointed towards the ferns. "Signal says we should go that way."

I didn't move my gaze. "Then let's go that way."

It was further than it looked. They trekked down through the jungle, arms up, on alert. The frost-trees were high above us down there. We approached the ferns, which looked more and more angular. I'd seen them before. I stopped and tossed a small rock at one; its fronds ratcheted high, creaking like old ropes, before a limit passed and the branch flared. Metallic spurs unfolded and the front struck, like a moving bear trap. Viper bush. The path through was pretty narrow.

I could hear the heavy swallows of the whole squad. "Fuck that," mumbled someone. Morale Boy and Mouth chattered about the viper bush. Incessant chatter, like old-school radios. *Radios. Like in terran choppers.* I sucked in some hot air, teetering; the connection on reality held. I turned back to Comms. "You really want to go through there?"

She checked her scope. "Getting close, Cap. Point one-one, bearing five degrees and minus four elevation. Right below us."

I looked around. I knew we were nowhere near the pod, but they didn't know that. Someone might make a mistake. And if we went higher, I'd have to pass some frost-tree trunks. I faced down the valley. "Fine," I said.

We skirted round each bush, in the halo where each had carved out its fellows. We dropped into more oppressive air. Mouth grumbled about saunas.

Finally, Comms pulled up in the lee of a stunted viper bush. "There," she said, pointing at one of the frost-tree megatrunks.

"Don't see a canopy break," said Morale Boy, scanning skywards.

"Can't be the pod then."

"Well, the signal ain't moving and it's connected to the game grid," argued Mouth.

So I wondered what it was. "You three with me. Rest of you, stay put."

I put the StrafeMaster between me and the giant frost-tree trunk. Inched forward. Didn't like getting this close. Its features resolved through the haze: the trunk was finned from ground to canopy, bulging at the base. Each fin was as thick as a thigh and had room for two men between them. The heat came in great waves; each one broke a fresh sweat.

"Wouldyalook at that?" muttered Mouth. "That's some crazy shit."

"Yeah, frozen up top and baking down here," said Morale Boy.

I was about to tell them to shut up when we came on a rumpled, prone, body-shaped mass. Mouth and I bumped heads over the body as we surveyed his gear. All-terrain suit with holographic camo. An empty holster for deconstruction munes; very fancy, and expensive. Didn't smell like a deputized combatant.

"Dead," said Mouth, poking at the body with his foot.

I shook my head, getting a really bad feeling. "If he was corpsified, his timepiece shouldn't be emitting."

"Well, maybe it's busted." And before I could stop him, Mouth poked at the timepiece. The ping from Comms's gear was immediate.

Under the vaulted canopy, I experienced one silent heartbeat. I knew what this was. My pulse jacked over one-seventy. Didn't want to be here.

Trap, I thought. And then I ran.

Most people think that in a firefight, there's noise and chaos. Shots ringing out, shit blowing up, men yelling above the maelstrom; but that's only for the cinefeeds. Tactical munes are molecular sharp and spat out of silenced accelerators in hypersonic range; they cut through without wasting energy making noise. And men under fire keep their yaps shut, too busy running or breathing, or laying low for sound. So I wasn't sure we were being fired on until the first guy went down. He crumpled in a red atomized cloud, puffed from the gaps between the wafer-useless body armor.

Comms, over the headset, was all I could hear. "Signal lock. Signal lock."

"Fucking jam it!" I was pressed against the earth, watching the puffs of dirt as the munes showered down the hill.

I pointed the StrafeMaster upground and let off a burst. Down came the monocle and the jungle reeled into overlayed spectrum. IR showed the hot trunks; UV lit the viper bush molecular machinery in cool blue. Some of the squad were down and not moving. Counted at least six. Memory-less now, lucky fucks. But there was nothing else to see. Confirmed my theory. I released the trigger and slapped the monocle away.

The others had found cover spots, but no one else had fired back. I could hear clicks, and swearing. "Malfunction, malfunction," began, and repeated. I tried to count them out; seemed no one had a weapon that worked, but I wasn't sure. I thought about vege spores choking the workings, or long-range jammers. Or just old, bad equipment.

A minute later came Comms. "They're off," she said. "Lock's gone."

Ten of us were left. I waited a while before I moved again, until the silence was too much to bear; the squad followed behind. "How many Deltas?" I heard someone ask Comms.

"That wasn't Deltas," I said. "It was a trap. A decoy body and a mune dispenser. Probably left from another game."

But still, it had taken out half the squad. Mouth, Comms and Morale Boy were all still there, so points off me for poor judgment. Maybe, I thought, just maybe I would make it.

Let Tartarus do the work.

Rain started, acidic stuff that stung all the scrapes and made the underbrush curl itself into hemispherical rocks. We tripped and stumbled down the last of the hill until it flattened and led to a drop-off: two sheer meters into a fault-line.

I went down into the soft mud and took a rest. I played with the SCM card, spinning it round between finger and thumb. The rest of them fiddled with their gear and weapons before they steadily gave up and sat down.

We were there a while; marking time in pretend sleep and distraction.

"Fucking mechanical shit," muttered Mouth eventually, collapsing in the dirt beside me. He was a software boy; hardware was clearly a puzzle. And it had been a long time since boot. I took the rifle off him. It took only a moment to disassemble. It had no firing bolt, so that explained that. I wondered whether to show him; I didn't.

"Hey, so, Cap? What GIMP block did you come out of?"

I took a breath. The question slammed a lot of memories into the chamber. Gray walls. Deep shadows. Invisible bars. Pain and solitary. Endless appointments. Rehabilitation. Nothing to make me forget. But I said, "E-one-nine-one."

Mouth whistled. "Wow, that's serious shit … treason, huh?"

I gave him a very dirty look.

"Hey," he said. "We're one-nine-ones too."

"Really."

"Yeah. Maybe—"

"Maybe you can stow it, Private. Bigger things happening here than what cell we sat in."

I got up and walked away. I pretended to watch the perimeter, but I was pretty spaced out. I could hear rotorbeats that I knew weren't there. I couldn't afford to lose it. That mem wipe was so close ...

Peripherally, I knew Morale Boy was helping Comms and three of the other grunts in rechecking their signal. As soon as they got a lock, we'd move again.

And that was when I lost it.

So sudden. Tartarus became a gray block command room. Peeling posters, a tangle of busted comms gear recovered from a chopper. *Two Charlie, two Charlie.* The Comms is sending, over and over, as blood slicks from his nose onto the console. *Mayday, mayday.* The dive room door is barricaded; it thumps. I walk behind Comms and draw my weapon. *Mayday, mayday.*

Somehow, I scrambled out. I swallowed the panic and counted out my breathes. Tartarus was back; so was the squad. It took a while to feel real again, the memory lingering like bitter tonic. I checked the timepiece; an hour had passed. I tipped my head back and let the tears run down my throat. I didn't want to go there again. Swore I wouldn't; just like the last time, and the time before.

And then I became aware the squad had drifted.

Down the fault-line, one of the frost-trees was right on the edge, its big fins sticking out over the crumbling rock wall, showing the deep, red-hot tap root punching down into the crust. Alongside were three dark bushes, elegant things, like bonsais of origami cranes. Three grunts were there, real close, checking it out.

I watched it happen; didn't move. The frost-tree shuddered and the next instant, the two grunts were gone. The trunk fins had closed, and flattened into a vice. One muffled shout made it out before a thick red splash came down the dirt. The third grunt stumbled sideways, coordination undone by what he'd seen. He tripped over himself and put a hand straight into the dark bushes. The whole lot collapsed. One moment, it was a Zen garden, the next, a broken card house. The grunt sat on his ass and stared at it.

Run, I thought, but I gave it no voice.

The crane-like pieces began re-assembly. They slunk over each other, angular edges articulated, and swarmed the grunt. His shriek cut off as the plume invaded his lungs. Flat out, mouth open, he became fertilizer stock. The bush reassembled over its new base, spreading in an elegant branch structure. Then all was still, like the event had been erased. *Nothing to see here.*

The remaining six squad stood, shocked. I remembered that realization, too. That everything here could eat you. That what seemed familiar was more alien and menacing than you could imagine. But at least here, I thought, when you were dead, that was the end of it.

But not everyone saw it that way.

Three grunts ran, straight down the fault, which left Mouth, Morale Boy and Comms with me and the carnage.

Mouth opened his. "Are those self-assemblers?" Morbid fascination.

I didn't answer. I watched the runners until they disappeared.

"Looks like," said Morale Boy. "Can't tell till they move. Fractal patterns, can you see? Probably stochastic, emergent behavior from simple rules."

I had no idea what fractals or stochastic was; I just wondered how long the runners had. But the three of them were staring at me, so I said, "Yeah, well simple rule is don't touch."

Several more of the bushes were collapsing and moving towards the one with the catch. I backed up, nice and easy.

Comms shifted her gear around and swore. "One of the runners had the bounce receiver."

I twitched my mouth. This made it easier. I knew from the SCM that they'd gone right towards the pod. "Guess we better see how far they can run."

Two hours passed; they'd gone a long way. We paced down the fault, keeping clear of the vege, tracking the footprints. Stopped to rest and started again. Mouth, Morale Boy and Comms kept pace pretty well for desk jockeys. But I tried not to feel attachment. Every step I worked on focus. I just needed to get out this time. Once more, and I was out. So I could do this. I could get through.

A headache descended, like it always did after a re-live; memory afterglow. It stayed an hour, and retreated, just as the air cooled. The canopy was thinning, letting in fresh atmo and harsh green-hued sunbeams burning up the foggy undercurrent. The edge itself was scalpel cut; branches and foliage ended in a neat line. The four of us stopped before we crossed it, just soon enough to save ourselves.

What was left of the three runners was laid out just beyond the edge. Well, pieces of them. I'd seen a lot of munes damage in my time, and this wasn't munes. I lifted my eyes. Not too far away was another tree-like thing, different from the frost-forest. Branches like zombie arms; massive reach. Trunk like an armored python. I knew the name of this one, but I'd never seen it.

"Weeping wraith," said Morale Boy, like he'd read my mind.

I lifted the StrafeMaster and slid my hands down the grip. I pushed the muzzle out; one inch, two. Sunlight touched barrel's end. There was a whisper hiss, and the tip fell. I stared at the slice of aerated metaloceramic, cut like a laser through grease.

Not even Mouth said anything. I pulled the monocle down and looked through the polarizer. In the spectrum view, I could see the tendrils. Morale Boy was rattling off about loops of atom-thin buckyrazor strings. About plant territorialism. A floating, near-invisible grid net. And a green zone just above the ground. All I could think was, there's only four of us left now.

Comms nudged me in the back. "Cap. Look."

And there, just visible in the wraith grove, was the goddam pod.

"They must have blasted a tunnel before they dropped it," said Mouth.

I didn't care what they'd done. It was the pod. The gateway to my mind-erase. It was cylindrical, crystalline; jammed into the ground on its drop spikes. Above all, I wanted to know that it was real.

I got down on my belly. Through the monocle, I could see the slice-n-dice tendrils wisping through the air. About two feet of air above the ground was clear.

I crawled. The pod was near the trunk; I went straight towards it, weaving through low scrappy bushes. Something they were exuding made my eyes water, but I didn't stop until I was beside the pod. Above, I saw the tunnel the gamemasters had made through the wraith. A safe zone. I stood up.

The pod seemed undamaged, and small, so small. The diamond panel over the control screen slid away in a well-oiled whisper. The screen was red: game still in play, and showing me exactly the same info the SCM card held. I ran my fingers over the pod's smooth shell, making it real.

Just one thing left to do.

A little track of cold sweat began at my nape and tracked its way south. I glanced back towards the frost-trees. With the polarizer on, Mouth, Comms and Morale Boy were just shadows behind the floating field of wraith fronds. My first thought was: what are the chances any of them were going to make it anyway? They'd have to come back two more times.

But one could make it now. The pod was real enough.

One could make it.

I looked down at the StrafeMaster, hanging from its shoulder strap. Memory was trying its reload again. They'd trusted me, back then, too, just like those three did now.

If I could have left, I would have.

Instead, I got their attention. Called them over.

I watched them come, hoping they'd make a mistake and the wraith would finish them first. But none of them did. Too soon, we were all by the pod.

"So, how's this work?" Mouth, naturally, had the screen cover off before I'd gotten my shit together. But maybe that was better. Forced my hand.

Mouth read the game type. "What's *Highlander*?" he asked. He looked back at me. Morale Boy and Comms too. A moment later, their hands slowly rose.

Because my StrafeMaster was up and ready. I inched the cut tip until it found the flesh at Mouth's throat. I felt him swallow. "It means," I said slowly. "That only one of us can leave."

"So, leave," said Mouth, his jaw making only small movements.

"Not going to stop you."

I had become flesh wrapped in sweat. "Sorry. Pod's not active until there's only one of us breathing."

I was going to do this. Had done it before. Once more: could do it again.

"Doesn't have to be this way," said Morale Boy.

Someone else said that to me once. *Then I see their eyes again, before I close a door and weld it shut.* I growled, and the memory retreated, but only just. I was shaking. "Yeah it does. Don't know why you volunteered for this, but you're not going to make it. So I'll make it easy."

Mouth's face twitches. Was he laughing? "What, you think we don't know what's going on? Stellines want us dead, Cap. If we'd stayed in the GIMP, they'd have had someone do it there. Couldn't stop us coming here, though. So, they're playing you to make it happen."

My eyes flickered.

"Don't you remember, Cap?"

I screwed my eyes shut. "I don't want to remember. So shut it."

Comms voice was low, and steady. "You should. Think about it. What did you do to get thrown in the GIMP?"

And so, we come back to now.

Two muddy feet, and fucking hesitation.

A memory reloads. I am back in the GIMP. In the gray-walled cell, with that Stelline psych. She touches her lips. I'm talking, like I didn't want to. *We were on recon*, I say. *Live planet. We didn't know about the alienoids. Squad got compromised. They didn't want to die.* Dimly, I feel the StrafeMaster in my hands, the pulse beating through the grips. *They were all done for*, I go on, talking through the memory. *The compromised turned on us. Our comms were short range. I didn't know anyone was coming for us.* And the psych's fingers linger on her lips. *You did what you had to do*, she says.

I snap back. Tartarus returns, green and deadly. Comms, Morale Boy and Mouth are all in my firing line. "I killed them. All of them," I say. "That's why I was in the GIMP."

I finger the trigger, but Mouth cuts in. "We had the same psych,

Cap. I hacked her records. That's how we met."

"Do you remember her, Cap?" asks Comms. "Do you remember what she told you?"

I can only remember one thing she'd said. "She told me I was still a man." My fists work the gun grips. "But she was wrong."

Comms is unmoved. "She said you were useful. She recommended you for special service. Because you're an easy trigger. We read the transcripts."

"I don't want to be useful. I just want out."

Mouth grins. "You're doing exactly what they want. Why else do you think you're the only one with a working weapon? That the gamemaster asked you for rank before he let you go with the SCM? We figured they'd do that. We figured how they'd play it."

This registers. Very slowly. A few sweaty seconds go by. *They played you*, I think. *They all played you from the start.*

"We have a better plan," says Morale Boy. "But we need you."

"The hell you do. Bad move. You read the transcripts, so you know my squad could have been treated. There was a treatment. They didn't have to die. And I killed them anyway."

Mouth takes a breath. "You had short-range comms, you said so. You only knew about the treatment later. You did what you had to do," he says, firmly. Like they know this already. Like they all understand how this is going to go, and I'm just catching up. A hostage drama with fucking reasonable hostages. I want them to lose it. Cry, beg, give me a reason. But they don't.

I finger the trigger. "I want out. I need that mem wipe. And the pod will only take one," I say.

Mouth glances towards it. "Cap, the pod's control is just software. And I'm good with that."

I narrow my eyes, and find myself arguing with them. "So, you get out. They'll be on you before you blink."

"So we have to hide. He's good with that," says Mouth, thumbing at Morale Boy. That third eye tat stares me down.

So I say, "They'll know where you've gone. They'll have a tail on you so fast—"

Comms puts a hand in her gear and pulls out the high-end EMP. "Signal scramble's a bitch with one of these things, Cap," she says quietly. "We have the means. Got it all. We need you."

"Why?"

"Because we wanna keep the stuff in our heads, and we can't shoot for shit. We need a field man. And we know you don't want to be a Stelline anymore."

"I won't be after this," I say. "I'm out and wiped clean. So I end you. I don't care if they wanted me to do it. I won't remember."

Morale Boy has a new expression and my sweat runs cold. "You really think they're going to let you out?"

"They have to. I've done three," I say, but doubt has pooled in the cold sweat. His expression is pity. Of all the nightmare memories shacked up in my brain, I never thought of this.

"We don't think so. Not a useful guy like you. They'll send you back. Do a partial wipe, maybe. They'll tell you it's just one more, then again, one more. Do you know how many times you've been here already?"

The statement makes the air heavy. My lungs struggle and my throat closes. A new headache hammers around my lumbering thoughts. I pull the trigger, but nothing happens. My body won't respond. Because somehow I know they are right.

The quiet passes for ten standard secs. Then Comms says, "You won't shoot because you like us. We worked hard on that. So you won't do it. We know you blame yourself. You don't want to do it again."

Some part of me is broken and unresponsive. I let Mouth push the StrafeMaster aside. My ass finds the dirt and the polarizer slips over my eye. I watch the wraith tendrils floating beyond the pod. I stare at the StrafeMaster barrel, resting on my thigh.

My thoughts remuster around a single idea. "I need a mem wipe."

Comms and Morale Boy exchange a look. "Cap, you've had the mems a long time. They might not go. Might be worse than now. But there's people we could go to," she adds.

I believe her for the time it takes them to go to work on the pod. Then I remember the doubt in her voice.

I watch them. They think they're right. Their activity is purposeful; a well-laid plan deep in execution. But I'm only useful if I remember my training, if I remember everything. So, they're never going to get me a wipe. They believe what that Stelline psych said.

They're all wrong.

I am not a man, not anymore. And I didn't tell them all of it; the one thing I never told the psych.

A memory reloads. *My gun against Comms' hair. A red spray. Another face, eyes shot with blood, then shot, more blood. They are all dead now, all except me. But I've seen my eyes in the latrine mirror; I'm compromised like the rest. I rest my gun on my teeth, but I can't do it. And it doesn't matter how much I tell myself I'm a coward; how much I know I should protect others from my infected form … I can't do it.*

Then finally, rotorbeats of rescue. A stolen treatment. But I'm compromised beyond the alienoid; I have no honor. I have survived, but I am no longer a man.

This is what I have to forget: the knowing I couldn't end myself after ending my own men. The knowing I thought I was strong enough, right until the last moment, when I wasn't.

Just like now.

The re-living loses time. When I come back, it's to the EMP burst and the pod in motion. Comms, Morale Boy and Mouth are busy with the controls. They're clever; they think they know me.

So I'm looking for another way out. Wipe that memory, so I can be whole again. Maybe I can do it.

Once more.

DEEP DECK 9

Login ☐ Sci-Bin004
Psswd ☐ ********
Awaiting Command☐ set_secure:ultra
Security set to ultra
Awaiting Command☐ recompile 06801A-Moon Ranger
Poseidon Sci-Bin004, DistComp subrtneJJ64
Sample extraction file retrieved
06801A
Begin recompile
     ****

They say space is a silent place to die, but I never worked out why. Sounds like something a planet-sider would say. Someone never been to space, never heard the sounds it makes.

Poseidon's curve is coming up big in the window, far too big for safety. But that's the general idea. It's a red and orange thumb-print, with its hazy gas-rock ring arching overhead. Civilization scars pock the surface; I used to live there, but it's never been home. And there's no time for nostalgia; the alarms will start soon enough. Smashed out a few but some I can't turn off; I already know we're going down. We're skipping into atmo too steep, moments from being a burning stone. And the ship thinks I need to know about things like that.

While the planet looms red and vast, my head is down in the floor, screwdriver rolling around on the GravDeck. I've barred the door, and I'm trying not to think about what's behind it. This is too important. They'll send the planet-side investigators for the crash-hardened black box after we've burned a long match-strike across

Poseidon's crust. So I'm digging down in the *Ranger*'s belly, going for the heart that holds those damn coordinates. The Junta can't find it.

They can't know where I've been.

Stitching non-concordant thought stream

Lou gave us the mission: a trunk call salvage twenty parsecs out. It was *us* then. Three tars and the *Moon Ranger*, just a standard fast shuttle with a DistComp: distributed computer inner skin. Just capable of the distance, and certainly capable of the desperate need to go. We owed Lou a favor, and no one usually survives owing Lou. I guess he keeps his rep.

A trunk call: that's what they call it when you're going beyond the comms limit, where a small problem overnights into a Poseidon-sized cluster-fuck. And this job was twenty parsecs past the asteroid shell, a celestial graveyard given up by Zeus' tidal pull. All the planets in this system are called by the old gods. The Junta thought that was a good idea; inspiring, nostalgic. Seems fitting to send the ship to die smashing into one of them.

Took two weeks to haul the *Ranger* out to the asteroid shell. There were stories about the shell. Find any old, red-wrinkled tar who's toasted too many mallows around old-school reactors and they'll tell you. The shell's a place for renegades, anarchists and secrets: for people wanting out of the reach of the planets. After the first decades of just hermits and the two-parts crazy, corporations took their out-of-regs research decks out into the shell. Must have been hard out there; lonely. Endless drone of recycled air; endless waiting between service drops, and endless deep, Cold Space. The real frontier. Men went crazy and topped themselves, and sometimes took the platform with them. But back within the comms, within the Junta's grip, there was no official word, only the stories.

So we never heard about Deep Deck 9.

At least, not until Lou did.

Stitching non-concordant thought stream

There's a shudder, and a red strobe blinks over my shoulder. That means the auxiliary life support's gone. The *Ranger*'s DistComp is keeping track of all this, and soon she'll warn me of last-chance-to-correct. Until then, she'll keep quiet. That's the good thing about the DistComp, and the difficult thing too. On the way back, after the others were gone, I thought about a quiet death. Blew the scrubber lines to pump monoxide back into the bridge, make the *Ranger* my last locker. But the DistComp is pretty clever, and odds are she'd get down on her own, even with me screwing the inputs. Can't let that happen.

Poseidon's tower is trying to raise me. Guess they're worrying I haven't noticed the trajectory. But I'll bet someone in the tower's got the *Ranger*'s signature off the transponder. They know it's me; I'm the best there is at course plotting, and sometimes I cut it fine for show. I won an award once, way back. I can bring any ship half-way across the system within a length of where you wanted.

That's why Lou gave me the job.

Stitching non-concordant thought stream

Everyone knew about the corporations in the asteroid shell, but Lou heard a whisper about Deep Deck 9 and did the kind of digging only he could do. Angelo Deep, entrepreneur, richest man in the systems. A man who'd started in the Junta but gotten exiled and made good elsewhere. A real pioneer, a *visionary* was what they called him. At least they did, three hundred years ago when he was last alive. The Deep Deck was launched from the shell, set in a long elliptical orbit and charged with a covert mission: new tech development, far from artful competitors. The Deck would spin out on its three hundred year orbit, and return with science built by a long-expired crew; on the vision of a man who wouldn't live to see it. Because a deck in Cold Space has no resupply; even with the best recyclers, you lose water and carbon until there's not enough left to run systems, until there's nothing to eat but polymer and chrome. Sending men out into that was real vision. No wonder Lou was impressed.

Of course, memory fades fast in this system. Too much happens in these tech-driven worlds and the Junta help some people forget. But Lou found it out: about the mission, and that the orbit was coming back close.

The window was tight. Twenty parsecs meant we had to cart

extra. Extra scrubbers, extra cyclers. We stripped the *Ranger* bare and had the extras crammed in every corner, and we still weren't sure we'd make it back. Fuel's not the problem once you're out on your delta-V. It's the air and water that'll bring you unstuck. The *Moon Ranger* doesn't have farms and processing of an interstellar freighter. So we had to stick it. Calculate the orbit on a bunch of guesses and hope. The plan gave us thirty minutes. Five to dock on and off, twenty on board. Twenty minutes to rip the spoils from the Deep Deck and bring them back for Lou. Twenty minutes on a four-week-plus turnaround was a drop in the starfield, and we all knew it. But we went.

The trip out to the shell was lots of nothingness. We watched re-runs, soaked the solar cells; Drake wrote his novel. Charlie paced and pretended to smoke. We passed through the shell, ports black like everywhere else with only the readouts to tell us we'd come within clicks of a hundred other unseen ships and stations. Then we were out into Cold Space, already beyond comms, beyond the *Ranger*'s rated limits. Drake and Charlie exchanged a look. They wouldn't have come but for me.

Now, they're gone anyway.

The morning we came up on the rendezvous, the DistComp began pinging after 0400. A lot of people don't believe in Old Earth time anymore. There was almost another coup about it on Poseidon, but the Junta put it down. They do things like that. I've got reason to remember; there's a chip in my head from fifteen years back. But I think we need things to hang onto in space. Time seems a small thing to keep.

After the alarms went off, we were up and quiet. I sat with my hand on the stick, but only out of habit. No one flies by wire on a course that long. If we were wrong, we were wrong two weeks ago, nothing to be done for it. Charlie drummed his fingers and stared out the bridge port. Not that there was anything to see. Drake didn't bother: the Deep Deck should have run out of critical gear within a hundred years without resupply, and the space bugs eaten out the solar cells. She should be dead black against black; we wouldn't see until she was right on us. Then *I see it* came croaking from Charlie's throat. Drake snorted; he thought Charlie'd lost it. Funny thing was: Charlie did see it. The Deep Deck came dead-on in the window, burning bright like a star in the field, like no station I've ever seen. Drake digested the apparition with a slow chewing motion, then slapped me on the back, credit for the navigation. But we exchanged the uneasy look that was due, the one that silently asked how a three hundred year old deck was still running hot, whether it would have air that was poison, or what kind of madness would be on board. Every Old Earth classic space movie feels real in Cold Space, so I was trying hard not to think of face huggers and sentient ships, and knew Drake and Charlie were doing the same. Not that anyone had ever found other life in the systems; that fact was enough to prop up some dying Poseidon churches, folded some others. But it didn't mean squat. Everything was real in Cold Space.

We locked on by 0408, started the timers, tested the comms and shouldered our salvage kits. We had twenty minutes to scramble before the Deep Deck dragged us out on her orbit, and it was three hundred years before someone else found our withered corpses stuck to her side. If we'd known then what would happen after, I wouldn't have cracked the airlock. I'd have broken away and pulsed the *Moon Ranger* straight back to Poseidon, and to hell with Lou. We should have trusted that deep pain in our guts. A ship *shouldn't* be running all bright and hot after three hundred years in Cold Space.

But we scented credit, and so we went.

We'd worried that the Deck would be a Tardis: ungovernable and unsearchable, needing Ariadne to make it back to the *Ranger*. But she wasn't. She was an antique with lots of molded plastic panels in her long, ordered tunnels, built before the verse went ceramic and silicon. The air was thick, but breathable, so we had our masks off in seconds. The Deck was pre-GravDeck: her magnetic drive tugged hard at the shoulder suits we'd brought.

And she was silent as a corpse.

We headed for the bridge. If the Deck was still running there was fair chance all the data was fresh. If it wasn't, we'd take only the solid-state memory and be done with it.

We passed endless windows showing lab space, all the glass frosty and glowing, benches bright white. Drake ran his fingers over surfaces and left no mark, which wasn't right. Even the *Moon Ranger* raises dust a few weeks from port, fine stuff that gets into everything. But the Deck was brushed bright, like it was new from Angelo's fab plant yesterday, not three hundred years in Cold Space. That was when we began to think there might be crew still here, or worse: another salvage ship with bigger thrusters docked round the back.

We reached the bridge in two minutes, empty beneath a yawning black sky port. Drake went for a console, found the keys fused, and plugged in another. It was the first sign the Deck was old, that this was real and not some Junta mind-spy trick.

There wasn't time to go hunting for physical spoils; information was the digital gold of the Deck, and we found it fast. Charlie pulled the solid-state data banks for system files, and the GhostDrive for the data. Twenty banks of solid-state meant nearly five-thou gig of data. The GhostDrive would hold five times more. In Angelo's time, GhostDrive was *new tech*; now, it was hideously obsolete, but we had it in under a minute. Thirty-thousand gig stolen in a few seconds. Enough to pay our debt to Lou.

Drake brought up the camera views, pocked and frosty. One by one they showed the ship, inside and out, up and down, and empty. And there was still sixteen minutes, time enough to look for more.

Drake and Charlie went. I stayed at the bridge and looked for the Deck's log, which since the beginning of the verse has been stored with HoloGen black box, somewhere on the bridge. Lou wouldn't want it; it wouldn't *sell*. I watched Charlie and Drake stride the long hallways, turning over trays in the labs. They stuck close, avoiding the quarters, recyclers, and plant rooms I saw from the frosty cameras. But they weren't finding much – the Deck was empty. No evidence of crew. Maybe there'd been one generation, maybe two or three. Lou said there'd been a hundred launched with the Deep Deck, enough for a few rounds of science kids who'd never seen planet-side before the supplies ran out. Kids didn't grow well off-planet. Didn't grow proper anywhere but Old Earth according to Lou. But what did Lou know.

Drake's voice came down the comms after five minutes.

"Creeps and crawls, boss," he muttered. "Can't hear the plant running."

"Power's on," I argued, thinking as much was damn obvious.

"'S'not running," he repeated.

"She's running on batteries then."

In the tiny camera view, Drake scratched his balls. You'd never know he wrote romances. "This old? Shouldn't be holding a charge at all."

"Yeah."

We all got the shivers. And with still ten minutes on our clocks we were heading back to the lock, feeling like we'd missed something. Charlie took the solid-state wafers in both hands and pockets, rubbing at his eyes with his shoulder. Drake had the GhostDrive, and I had the HoloGen black box under my arm. The data was Lou's, but any man had the right to take something he thought might sell from a salvage. Or a trophy he wanted to keep. If Drake and Charlie took anything, I didn't see it.

We were dusted by 0430. I watched the Deep Deck's bulk pull away into Cold Space, still glowing bright like festival lights.

And there, as Drake and Charlie turned away, I was sure I saw them.

Faces, hundreds, pressed against the sub-deck windows. Staring with blank white eyes; slack-jawed leers and slashed skin. Looks I'd seen in a Zeus dope house. One moved, jerking. I froze, squinting as the pulse drive engaged. But as we streaked away I couldn't be sure. I was damn glad for every parsec fraction between us, and glad it would be another three centuries before anyone would get close.

Except that wasn't the end.

I had to knuckle-to for an hour: check the course plot for the two-plus week haul back to Poseidon while a correction was still possible.

Then, we got into the data.

Drake couldn't resist a peak, no salvager can, really, even when the goods don't belong to you. For the measly hours or days the stuff is in your possession, you want to know what you bought for the other guy with your sweat and adrenaline. Pays to know what he owes you, or in this case, to be sure we were even again.

So we cracked out the solid-state, asked the Deep Deck for her secrets.

She was a research platform. Drake snorted as Charlie made the proclamation. Anyone could see that. Charlie blushed. Multidisciplinary, which surprised us at first. On Poseidon, the regs restrict corporations to one industry, been like that for as long as anyone can remember. In the early days, it stopped the massive enterprises with lots of capital being the only ones who could afford a foot out into the space systems and gave the Junta more control. But no one really thought it out, 'cause it just meant the deals went below ground. Business as usual. And it helped men like Lou become big. They're the dealmakers, setting up arrangements between the biotechs and the med-scis; genetics researcher needing neuroscience? They'd fix you up. Nothing traceable because they did nothing themselves; webmasters for information and contacts. But the Deep Deck was before all that, and there weren't any regs in Cold Space.

The Deck's specs were all laid out in the solid-state. She'd had bio-labs, cryos, cyberface and astro-geo fabricators, soft condensed matter, nanoetchers and hi-funk computer power.

But we couldn't find the mission plan, and no logs for research objectives. I'd done a couple of hits on research labs over the years, and that was a first. Charlie frowned, furrows etching deeper as he skimmed the docs. Eventually, Drake got bored and went back to his novel. I sat under the star panel, and the soft whiz of Charlie scanning through kept me company into sleep.

Charlie woke me hours later with a shake, his hand cold from hours outstretched on the track ball.

"I worked it out," he said softly. A blinking green LED lit up his wild eyes. I was awake pretty fast.

Charlie led me back to the *Ranger* comms, his words coming in spurts, blocking and unblocking as his thoughts gave way in a tumble. "You can't get a sense of it, not unless you look real wide, right? Well, but it's in there you see, like, between the lines? What they *don't* say, that's the important thing."

"Say what you mean, Charlie."

The sight of Drake rubbing his ugly face injected more clarity.

"There was no mission plan," said Charlie slowly.

"We know that," said Drake, impatient.

"On purpose."

Drake snorted. "You wake me up for this?"

Even I smiled a bit, but Charlie, for once, wasn't deterred.

"They did it as a *Push*," he hissed. A hand whizzed off into space in illustration. Drake's face fell with mine.

"You sure, Charlie?"

Charlie nodded fervently. We sat him down.

A Push was an experiment the Old Earth military Juntas did when the space systems were new. Took a bunch of guys up by force, set them off in space. No mission, just supplies and random crap, and forgot to mention there was no return. Then, the Junta's sci-boys would start their fun. They'd fail the life support or the GravDeck, just to see what happened; some were told their family was being held. Then, at some critical moment, the sci-boys would tell the crew they were on their own.

Pushes were supposed to log character traits necessary for life in the space systems, but anything could happen. Bunch of desperate men in a boat means complex dynamics. Ships were lost. There was anarchy and suicide and kamikaze vengeance crashes. One crew brought their spacerunner down on the Apollo tower. There's still a crater there. As a program, Pushes were spectacular failures, but the sci-boys were fascinated. Their models expected different results. Then the planet-side journos got wind of it and public pressure shut them down … or at least, made them quiet. But that was Earth. The Junta on Poseidon still flaunted the occasional Push on its books. For political prisoners, or a threat to anyone they wanted silenced. Charlie's dad had gone on one, way back. That's one reason Charlie's the way he is. Almost got myself thrown on one years ago after I salvaged some secrets the Junta didn't want known; instead, the sci-boys put a chip in my head so I can't remember what I found. Guess I was lucky.

But the Deep Deck being a Push was weird. A Push was always done with an old ship, not far from decommission. Even the Junta didn't waste new infrastructure on something that would likely crash and burn. And the Deep Deck had been better than new; it was new and *expensive*. Best equipment. A Push didn't make sense … except if they'd counted on a rare exception. Sometimes, the Push environment drove people into a higher state: bonded, efficient, unstoppable. Of all the Pushes, Charlie only knew of two like that. One where the guys brought their ship back to planet-side and emerged telepathic. Who knows what the Junta did with them. And another where the crew handed the Junta a gift: the *Jefe* raised his eyebrows and no one saw them again.

All this passed between Drake and me in an instant, but Charlie was already working the track ball, showing us the systems architecture, the setup, the personal diaries. And it looked like a Push alright. A bunch of top-class sci-boys with no mission sent off into Cold Space.

I got a cold wash when I understood Angelo's vision. No one could claim they were just following orders. Instead, the strongest would win; progress and invention would be born and die to keep Cold Space out, and prevent it from eating the minds of all on board. And if it didn't work, it would crash and burn like all the others. But out in Cold Space, no one would know or remember. Angelo Deep's vision was fairly cut with crazy. Lou would love it.

"So what the hell did they come up with?"

We all turned to stare at the GhostDrives, but I had to put the idea down. GhostDrives were old tech and finicky.

"No. That's Lou's problem. We don't jack 'em here. If they're blank, he can't claim it was us that wiped it."

"If they're blank, he'll jack us anyway," complained Drake. But no one moved. No one was going to risk a GhostDrive in the dirty *Moon Ranger* ports.

"That why there wasn't anyone there? 'Cause of the Push?" Charlie said.

"Been three hundred years, Charlie."

"Yeah."

"Drake, you see anything when we was there?" Charlie asked in a small voice.

Drake shook his head. "Creepy but. The plants weren't runnin'."

"Yeah."

Charlie didn't ask me, so I didn't say anything. Even if I had, don't think it would have changed things.

We coasted back through the shell without activity on the comms. People who go out there don't do it to talk to others, and the company decks don't advertise they're there at all. Then three days through warm space, on course for Poseidon and Lou's hovel. We were still more than a week from planet-side, and about as far from help as you can imagine. Maybe they knew that.

Charlie came to see me just after the lights went down. We keep a 25-hour light cycle on board; a poor attempt to emulate hardwired circadian rhythms.

"Boss." Charlie only calls me that when he's really distressed. When he forgets that he's not supposed to sound like Drake, 'cause Drake doesn't like it.

"What, Charlie?"

Charlie sat down on the edge of my bunk, rubbing his hands over his face. He was the gray of a sleepless man, but he couldn't start himself talking.

"What, Charlie?" I said again.

"I think I'm seeing things."

"What things?"

Charlie looked up at the ceiling, where a loose panel hung from three corners, showing the bright radiation shield behind. He rubbed at his eyes as he spoke. "Something ain't right. Could have sworn, when we was on the Deck… I saw something funny… and now, well, something like the same. These ghosty things, here a moment, then gone again."

"Charlie?"

He looked at me then, an empty cavernous look, eyes blank and staring. It made me pause. Charlie was a funny character, but looks like that don't come from a person. It was a *thing* that made it; more basic than a person, more fundamental. A look of raw yearning, calculating for a primal need and deciding whether to kill you for it. I've seen that look before, but never in a man's eyes. Charlie shook his head and the look was gone.

"Boss," he croaked finally. "Did you see anything, out there?

On the Deck?"

I'm not in the habit of lying. "Couldn't be sure, Charlie. Maybe, but not till we were off anyways, even then I couldn't be sure what it was."

Charlie nodded, staring out the port into the big black. "Can we check the tapes?" he said.

That was bold for Charlie. The surveillance buffer was held on the Deck's HoloGen black box. HoloGen's run a buffer, but only actually record significant events, which includes the black box being removed, so it would show our salvage. But the HoloGen was my prize, and no one ever put a hand on someone else's goods. Charlie would never have asked, the Charlie I knew. That should have been my first clue.

But I said, "Sure, Charlie."

We went through every feed, watching ourselves and the otherwise empty Deck, three times through. We saw nothing.

"Maybe we should try—"

"Again," said Charlie.

I sighed and reloaded. One more time. An hour later, Charlie got up and I watched him go. That's when I caught it; just at the corner of vision. If I didn't look directly at the screen, I saw a blip in the frame rate, like creases in feed, a presence hidden under some kind of cloaking. They were there all the time: those *things* I'd seen in the port as we'd pulsed away from the Deck. One followed Charlie as he moved through the labs, a holographic shadow touched him while he picked up some tubes. Another traced Drake as he opened a cupboard, lifting a book in a thermaseal case. Ah, fuck, they were everywhere. The whole time they'd followed, shadowed, touched. My stomach volunteered for a turn-out, and I had to look away, swallowing.

I had no idea what the hell they were. I watched myself on the bridge, but there weren't any hovering shapes there.

Then, I got a crawling sensation, enough to make me look around.

Charlie stood over me, frozen, his face blank and fixed. He had a galley knife in his hand and drool slicked in a long string from his mouth. He wiped his mouth slowly, and stared at the knife like he didn't know what it was.

"Charlie?" My voice shook, a rare thing.

Charlie put the knife on the table slowly, then sat. Blinked twice. "Hm?"

"What are you doing?"

He looked up and down, confused. Went white, like he might vomit. "Think I'll go and lie down, boss."

"Good idea."

I got Drake.

While Charlie slept, we cracked the GhostDrive. Drake drank cup after cup of the foul brown liquor he's fond of. I just got high on the fumes. The research logs were long and stopped suddenly eighty years after the Deck's launch. Long before that, the entries acquired a Cold Space-soaked lingo that made it new-space Dutch to me. But Drake was educated. He worked it out.

"They locked them in there, you know," he said.

"In the Deck?"

Drake looked around to see if Charlie was back. He wasn't. "Yeah. They didn't tell 'em about the Push. They brought 'em out here, told 'em it was a job in the shell maybe. But then, they boosted the Deck and left 'em there. That's what I reckon."

"Yeah?"

"No thrusters. Anywhere." Drake tapped the plant layouts. "So no steering, no orbit change. Committed and helpless."

I shuddered. "Wonder who they pissed off."

"The sci-boys? I don't reckon they did nothin', 'cept being the best at all this shit."

"Why waste them on a Push, then?"

Drake didn't answer but laid out the Deck's starting streams. He showed me how all of them – the biomeds, nanotech, physiology, psychology, microgravity – had run together and become indistinct from the sci-boys themselves. There was one all-consuming objective: to get out. They'd tried every angle to change themselves … viruses, machines, pharma … ways to be consumed and remade, remembered and reformed, over and over. Trying to become something that would last.

Drake rubbed his eyes. Squinted at the dregs in his cup. Rolled his tongue around like he'd just noticed the liquor tasted foul.

"Those smart sci-boys and all their tech on a Push means you're probably gonna get high-tech fighters out of it, right?" he said. "I mean, biomed, nanotech, physiol, all that stuff ... Angelo probably expected they'd finish up self-experimenting. Might make sense if you wanted trooper mods, like the Junta does. But what I don't get? Why the hell would you do it on a Push for three hundred turns? What comes back might not want to play no more."

Yeah was all I could say.

Drake glanced around again, looking for Charlie, then stared me right in the eye. "Why would Deep do it? I mean, the Junta hated him, right? Why try to make something they could steal?"

I didn't know.

"If it was you," said Drake. "Whadda you reckon you'd want if you got out after all that time?"

We looked at each other.

"Revenge," I said, feeling a cold wash replacing Drake's liquor in my guts.

Stitching non-concordant thought stream

Finally, the alarms are going. There's two — one slow whoop for the approach vector, one rapid bleep for the life support. That means in twenty clicks, the DistComp will mayday the tower and take over.

She can try.

By then, the *Ranger* will be a heartless shell, spinning helpless towards Poseidon, because I've got the black box. It's the size of my thumb, wires adangle.

I hear dragging footsteps out in the passage, steps made on inhuman legs. A dull wet thump counterpoints the steps. Then there's a metallic crash against the door.

He's found a tool then. *It*. It's found a tool.

And I've got to worry about that, because Drake was always smarter. And that seems to make a difference.

Stitching non-concordant thought stream

Charlie never came back from his bunk. Drake went to look about 0930 and didn't find him. We started a watch.

We were all strung up, expecting attack, but we didn't see it coming.

Without so much as a photon out of place, Drake took a heavy hit, went down fast. The thing that had done it flickered, and I saw it.

It was Charlie.

Or at least, something like Charlie. It stood leering, teetering, fixing Drake with one white eye. The moment stretched eternal as I saw: flesh hung from the other eye socket in stringy threads. His fingers were moth-eaten, knuckles split to the bone with the skin dry and raw.

The white eye swiveled round to me. The thing reached out, and stumbled. I choked on an acid heartbeat and went for the door. By then, once-was-Charlie was vanishing again, his skin going milky then clear. The transparency wavered as if Charlie was fighting against whatever was taking over his body. He took two steps, then fell through the door face first, ending up unconscious on the GravDeck.

My body moved without me, doubling back for the bridge where we keep the arms all salvagers carry. I closed the bridge port and went to Drake. He breathed shallow; where his head had hit the wall was a bloody spot like a sun. I shook an Armor Special from the arms locker, felt the barrel's weight. Approached the second port with the Armor cocked and ready.

But Charlie was gone. I kicked around the floor. Not just invisible. Gone.

Not knowing if the thing was already inside, I sealed the bridge and changed the door codes. Did a sweep, passing down the passageways like marine guys I'd seen on the telefeeds. Around corners, barrel out. Scared shitless but desperate.

Nothing.

Charlie'd done a runner, probably holed up in some hull crack. I got to thinking, and I reckoned Charlie passing out had been the last of his will power. Next time we saw him, there'd be no trace of *him* at all. So I went back to the bridge and got sealed inside. Only then did I check the Armor. Not loaded. Fuck. And no ammo in the arms locker. Cold Space settled in my stomach; there'd been ammo there when I opened it. And Drake was still out cold. No-longer-Charlie had been back while I was away and swiped it. That's when the pings started for planet-side approach. Talk about fucked up timing. Poseidon was still several hours and we had a problem to contain. I got tools and started ripping panels.

Stitching non-concordant thought stream

The black box is ended, boot-shaped dent in it. I shredded the HoloGen and the GhostDrive with a plasma cutter. Can't have Lou getting profit outta this. But there's still the *thing* behind the door. The planet-side research bins are pretty sharp, they'll try to study it. So if it gets down, it'll be out, no question.

Stitching non-concordant thought stream

Drake woke eventually. Came round groggy, one pupil fixed and dilated. He didn't make much sense. But I knew what he was trying to say. That we were rooted and never going home. That the Deep Deck's tech was taking over. Something superior, a survivor. He mumbled about picomachines and reworking the body. About regeneration and spreading, things I hadn't read in the logs but he had. In a conscious moment, he railed about the sci-boys on the Deck; that whatever was left of them hadn't come with us because the *Moon Ranger* was too small for mass escape, but they could send agents. So, if I landed, it would be as one of them, and the rest of the verse to follow. I told myself he was damaged, that he wasn't making sense, but he was.

I did another sweep once those pings came on, buoyed up on a swig of Drake's brew. I wanted to know what lurked in the *Ranger*; I wanted to end the problem. I wanted to believe I was going home.

I found Charlie. He was lying on the GravDeck, near his bunk. He'd taken a knife to his face and gouged out his temple, soft pink brain dripping red into a puddle. Made me think of strawberry sauce at a Poseidon candy bar, so I spent a minute heaving up nothing on the GravDeck.

And Charlie had done it all right. One last courageous act. I told Drake, and he mumbled about disinhibition. He said the disassemblers started in the front of the brain, where they could start pulling apart. Drake reckoned that's why Charlie was seeing things, why he'd gotten bold. The things got in through the eyes, optic nerve like a pipe to the brain. And as they went, the disassemblers couldn't avoid setting off signals. Then, they got into the frontal lobes: undoing the brain parts that keep you socially in line. Eventually, it would remodel everything it wanted. That's why the skin looked all raw and dry. Wasn't cut up at all, just being stripped for parts one angstrom at a time. The Deck sci-boys must have thought they were immortal, but once your brain gets taken over, there were no rules anymore.

I didn't touch him.

But I got to thinking about why the thing would try to kill Drake. Ah. I stopped. Got a notion: bold Charlie, knows he's done for, but tries to kill Drake, the smartest guy on the ship. Because he knows the things are already working on Drake.

I got the cold chills again, but this time, the ones that come when you know you're alone and being hunted.

Went back to the bridge.

The gun was gone. And so was Drake.

Stitching non-concordant thought stream

He's gone quiet out there but I can hear the keypad bipping as he pushes keys. I'd shut down the system, but the doors failsafe to open. And even without the *thing*, there's not much air out there, and I won't choose to suffocate. That's a joke around the ship ports. Way back, when the boats were first on the ocean, a sailor's death was drowning. Now, out here, it's bug-eyed death in the vacuum.

It's the one thing I can't face.

Stitching non-concordant thought stream

With Drake gone, I finally believed him. The Deck things hadn't taken the *Moon Ranger* when we were docked because they weren't stupid. A lot changes in 300 years, and not enough spots for all to escape, so safer to keep the crew human until they knew where they were bound. They'd sent an agent, or *agents*: parasites. To make more of them. What the plan was from there, who knew. Rescue mission? Takeover? It didn't matter.

I blew the life support lines. Anything I could jettison from the bridge, I tripped. Air went rushing out of the *Ranger*, all but the bridge bubble. For a few minutes, I thought I'd done some good, but the footsteps started up.

Like a dead man, slow and steady.

Drake was far beyond needing to breathe so much. The undead don't need it.

I thought about snuffing out. Not suffocating exactly; I'd let the core monoxide bleed back into the bridge. Breathe my way to quiet cherry-red death. He was going to get in here anyway, and there was nowhere else to go.

I got as far as the final switch, a big red fucker marked with DANGER: MAINTENANCE USE ONLY. Then I paused for comforting routine, and ran my fingers over the re-entry checks, which made me look at the hull cams: I saw a bright buff around the life support exhaust pipe. Now, ceramometalic ship hulls like the *Ranger*'s get a space patina: a dull skin shot-peened by tiny flakes of this and that, and slow planet-side oxidation. But the metal around that pipe was bright and glowing, like the *Ranger* was a clean-skin again, fresh from the assemblers, not five decades in service. Just like the Deep Deck, scrubbed clean with pico-who-knew-what-machines. The things were beyond just *us*. They had the *Moon Ranger*, headed for Poseidon. Where there's a thousand other ships, and thousands more hapless tars like me.

So I tipped the entry too deep, and set a trap inside the door. Got my heavy tools out and went hunting for that black box so no one could trace us back. The only problems now are the Junta and Lou. Because there had to be nothing left to tempt them, and if any fragment of the DistComp survived, they'd have the answer and send another mob. Pull out the stops and find a bent ship with bigger boosters than the *Ranger*.

They might just make it.

*** Stitching non-concordant thought stream ***

The keypad entries get slow and deliberate. I think Drake is fully gone now, the *thing* just riding on what's left of his gray matter. And the Armor's out there too, though somehow I doubt he'll use it. I know he's after me alive. Another body to infect. Become a dead host for pico-assemblers, hive machines with an appetite for brain and a hunger for revenge.

Bip. Bip. Bip. Bip. He's trying combinations in order now. Pity;

in the reset I hurried and set 0-0-0-3.

So two more goes and the door shoots open with a burst of flame: Drake's liquor in its only useful function. A fireball flares around an invisible mass. Drake flickers visible. His skin lights in places, but mostly it just glows bright. Raw flesh hangs from his neck, flames leap through the gaps.

The heat mixes with the hot cabin air, rushing out into the void. It stumbles forward.

The ship shudders. Alarms are going off everywhere. I silence them all and they become red flashes on my retinas. I put my hands on the *Ranger*'s controls. Outside the port, the air glows: white hot plasma superheating in our stream. The ceramic won't last much longer.

Something cracks.

In my rear-view, Drake's white eyes go to the instrument panel, then to my throat.

But it's too late.

The port streaks and melts. Thick hot air burns my insides.

The thing in Drake knows it's too late, but it comes on anyway.

There's time to think silent apology to the *Moon Ranger* for this death, before a ragged, half-seen hand grips my throat. Before the tingling invasion of disassemblers burrows into my jaw. One more host. A chance to survive the crash.

But I'm the best there is at course plotting.

She cracks again, and the bridge is a plasma hot breath. My body's gone, silent, a captain's death.

But the last thought is hope. That Lou doesn't send another team. That this ship burns so nothing's left. That the Deep Deck finds a comet on her long orbit, or some other means of destruction. That she's not still there when the Poseidon system expands itself into Cold Space, ready for invasion.

* * * * * * * * * *
End. Recompile terminated near subject expiry.
Neural Ship Log on chip series 0041-A.
Recompile:0426 Poseidon Sci-Bin004 DistCompsubrtneJJ64.
Subject: Parker, J.
File 06801A-Moon Ranger
Awaiting Command□

More from Charlie Nash

Four original stories of cyberpunk, steampunk and post-apocalyptic inspired fiction, including the award shortlisted "Alchemy & Ice". Available in print and digital.

Seven original fantasy stories with a dark twist, including the multi-award shortlisted slipstream experience "The Ghost of Hephaestus". Available in print and digital.

Printed in Great Britain
by Amazon